Tales of Eltham

Eltham Park South

St John's Church - Eltham

Copyright © 2014

All authors retain copyright of their short stories.

ALL RIGHTS RESERVED. This book contains material protected under International and Federal Copyright Laws and Treaties. Any unauthorized reprint or use of this material is prohibited. No part of this book may be reproduced or transmitted in any form or by any means, electronic or mechanical, including photocopying, recording, or by any information storage and retrieval system without express written permission from the author / publisher.

Layout and Design by Andy Grachuk © 2014
www.JingotheCat.com

THIS BOOK IS DEDICATED TO MRS MAUREEN SANDERSON, WHO WROTE HER ELTHAM STORY BUT SADLY DIED, AGED 80, IN MAY 2014 BEFORE THIS BOOK WAS PUBLISHED.

Contents

Friendship, Love and Loss
A Letter to Pete by Sue Head	*16*
See you soon, Stan by David Culver	*17*
Target minus 20 minutes by Pam Percy	*18*
Fish by Margaret Lewis	*19*
An accomplished life continued by Alex Farrow	*20*
Goodbye James by Dana Wiffen	*21*
Solo Sausages Again by Barbara Scott	*22*
Football in the Park by Sue Williamson	*23*
First Love by Shaheen Westcombe	*24*
The Man with the Grey-Striped Shopping Bag by Aylia Fox	*25*
Bang! by Jasmine Alvis	*26*
A Past Eltham Love by Julie Bartley	*27*
Off-road by Tom Ryan	*28*
The Butterfly Garden by Jane Chandley	*29*
Marriage at the Barn by Jamie Byrnes	*30*
Hope by Melek Ibrahim	*31*
Remember by Ann Tolladay	*32*
Dress Code: Poirot	*33*

Memories
Last Ride on 'The Eltham Flyer' 5th July 1952 by Ernest Jupp	*38*
A Warm Welcome to Coldharbour by Dawn Winchester	*39*
One hit Wonder by Sarah Smith	*40*
A Minor Success by Geoff Lander	*41*
Our Dream House by Elisabetta Pancucci	*42*
A Royal Encounter by Jill Lee	*43*
My Soul still Rests at Eltham Palace by Anne Sharman	*44*
A Tale from Eltham Green Comprehensive School by Shirley Fox	*45*
From Pantomime to Poltergeist by Paul Cookson	*46*
Last Swim by Jill Carr	*47*
Ted's Journey by Luke Edeson	*48*
Your Faithfully, Eltham by Alex Wingham	*49*
The Rich Scoundrel By Teresa Nash	*50*
A Link to Eltham's Past by Spencer Drury	*51*

Queenscroft Park 1980 by Sheila Bishop	52
The Solo by Linda D'amiral	53
Terror in Eltham 1952 by Chris Almond	54
My Misspent Youth by Mick Cohen	55
In Some Corner of a Foreign Field by Luke Carter	56
We used to go Dancing at Burtons by Chris Page	57
Palace Prediction by Mark Wall	58
Health and Safety by Hugo Robinson	59
My life in Eltham by Maureen Sanderson	60
Cold Hands by Miriam Storey	61

Our Animal Friends

Eltham Escape by Beatrix Robinson	66
Little James, the Giant Mole and Cannibal Pigs by Tony Tang	67
Funeral in Eltham by Val Spargo	68
Mah-Jongg's Journey by Doreen Thorogood	69
Eltham Pantomime by Paul Harton	70
Eltham Reserve by Liz Davies	71
A Babe in Eltham Park North by Frances O'Connor	72
Cats and Dogs! by Tessa Cheek	73
Wolfy and Jessica by Annalise Webber	74
Queenscroft by Antonia Robinson	75
Am I imagining? by Georgie Hawkins	76
The Rustle in the Tree in Eltham by Katie Geogiou	77
The Friendship Ponies by Kaelyn Okai	78
Found in Eltham by Sofia Drake Perella	79
The Mystery Cat by Natasha Wren	80

A Victorian Murder 1871

April is the Cruellest Month by Reeva Charles	86
The Eltham Case by Joanne Walby	87
Wading through the Dewy Grass by Isabella Fuller	88
The Ghost of Kidbrooke Lane by Koren Ozmus	89
25th April 1871 by Maisie Hook	90
The Spirit of Jane! by Sinem Ozturk	91
It was a Dark and Windy Night by William Quilter	92

Ghosts and Fantastical Goings On

The Ghost of Eltham Church by Liam Fitzpatrick	98
CTRL - ELT - DEL by Anna Cookson	99
The White Bus by John Wingham	100
The Montbelle Ghost by Alan Moc	101
The Funfair by Amina Khan	102
The Ghost of Eltham by Arran O'Leary	103
Billy and Alice's adventure by Brooke Francis	104
Molly's Dream Comes True by Caitlin Barcoe	105
The Haunted Room! by Chelsea Williams	106
Mrs Almond? by Demmie Jacobs	107
The Ghost of McDonalds by Francis Tweneboa - Koduah	108
Ghosts by Gabriele Zebrauskaite	109
Ghost night of Eltham by Jonathan Abbott	110
The Haunted Museum! by Kayley Hayward	111
Jack and the Ghost in Eltham Palace by Michael Tweneboa- Koduah	112
The Haunted Library by Molly Piller	113
The Tidal Wave by Nathan Mansfield	114
The Murder on the Train by James Double	115
Ghost in the Graveyard by Yad Abdullah	116
Alien by Zaina Kadir	117
Eltham by Zohra Amiri	118
The Time Machine by Cara Cloke	119
The Boy Who Got Blasted into Space by Joseph Cerda	120
The Secret of Eltham's Fairies by Marianne Robinson	121

Eltham Life and Miscellany

The Music and Movement of a New Mum by Alex Farrow	126
The Move by Pat Duffy	127
Awake Again by Angela Sach	128
My Story by Jack Warde	129
Trick or Treat? by Heaven Osmani	130
Resolution by Roberta Woods	131
Help??? by Ruby O'Connor	132
An Eltham Party by Molly Warde	133

FORWARD

It felt a real privilege to be one of the judges of the Eltham short-story competition in 2014 for which the stories in this collection were written. My colleagues and I from the University of Greenwich, Faculty of Education and Health learned so much from reading stories written by the adults and children from Eltham. Importantly, all the stories shared a character – Eltham itself. The town's presence in the tales you are about to read unites all the authors in an important way and makes this collection unique and valuable.

Short story writing is often said to be the most difficult of all prose forms of fiction. The best short story writers need to apply masterly craftsmanship combined with a love for form and an unerring eye for drama, all of which needs to be balanced with an instinct for simplicity and is expressed in a style that is lucid and concise. To the authors' credit, many of the stories have been able to accomplish these traits; indeed, the authors had a particularly special challenge of writing a story in no more than 300 words. Try it for yourself; this is not at all an easy accomplishment!

The stories in this collection are often a delight to read and many will move you with the strength of the emotions that are expressed within them. Many of the stories centre on the lives that have been lived in Eltham and the events that shaped them. Many are steeped in history and the people that make Eltham such a unique and special place. Some of the authors have used interesting forms to tell their tales. One, for example uses a letter to tell the story of a heartfelt remembrance of a 'love from long ago'. The best manage to avoid being over sentimental by a lightness of touch to the storytelling. Many of the stories have real poetic qualities and find jewels of language to use to delight their audience. Readers will also meet a lovely sense of humour in many of the works which some will say is special to Eltham and its people.

The language arts are alive and well in Eltham and this book of short stories crafted by local people is a tribute to all those who wrote for the short-story competition and the people and places that provide the substance of these engaging tales.

Professor Andrew Lambirth
University of Greenwich
August 2014

Introduction

Eltham is now a suburb of London. It has a history stretching back at least to the time of the Romans. It has a splendid royal heritage with Eltham Palace being the childhood home of Henry VIII and the 16c Tudor Barn being the home of Margaret Roper, the daughter of Sir Thomas Moore.

However, Eltham has been home to generations of people who have all experienced life here and absorbed the history. In 2013, people were asked to write poetry about Eltham and 'A Celebration of Eltham in Verse'* was created.

Eltham needed another challenge! In 2014, people were invited to write about 'an Eltham Experience' for a community short story competition. The story could be fiction, non-fiction or a mixture of both! The challenge was 300 words and set in Eltham. Many people met this challenge, and what a great response from children and adults.

We had stories related to Eltham's rich history, some with a modern day twist. We had memories of life in Eltham, funny stories and stories of love and friendship. Eltham may have it's 'real' ghosts, but the fictional ghosts in Eltham must make it a hotspot for strange goings on.

The Tales of Eltham have been divided into chapters with an introduction for each chapter. You may or may not know the people and places but as you read them Eltham will become familiar to you.

The Tales of Eltham are each inspired by an Eltham Experience. They have been written from the imagination and memories of people who know Eltham and have shared their creativity. Read and enjoy them!

Gaynor Wingham
Eltham Arts
August 2014

* A Celebration of Eltham in Verse by Gaynor Wingham (ISBN: 9781491236710)

Acknowledgements

Thank you to our sponsors and supporters of the Tales of Eltham Competition including :

Conran Estates, University of Greenwich, Royal Greenwich Libraries (GLL), Metropolitan Police, Greenwich Visitor, the White Hart, and everyone from the local schools, businesses and community organisation.

Thank you to the competition judges from Greenwich University Faculty of Education, Royal Greenwich Libraries (GLL) and the local community:

Andrew Lambirth, Susanna Steele, Penny Smith, Sarah Smith, Roger McDonald, Julia Hall, Gordon Ade Ojo, Amanda Henshall, Paula Bellamy, Scott Landers, Michael Kelpie Rebecca Gediking and James Benmore.

A special thank you to my husband John, son Alex, Amy Duffin and Andrew Lambirth for supporting me throughout this project and the Eltham Arts Committee for making all this possible.

Copyright : Gaynor Wingham

All authors retain the copyright of their short stories.

Photographs courtesy of the Gaynor Wingham Collection ©2014

1910 - Greetings from Eltham

Friendship, Love and Loss

Friendship, love and loss have been a source of powerful inspiration to writers over the centuries. Eltham writers were able to describe in many different ways what relationships meant to them and stories tugged at many heartstrings. The winner of the adults category for our competition was Sue Head's short story 'A Letter to Pete'. A story based on a teenage experience of love and loss which we can all identify with, written in a moving, yet concise, way.

Some recall loss by death and others a brief meeting which impacted on a life and left an emotional hole. A reunion through social media, a lonely hearts date and a singles night at a local supermarket inspire stories.

There are stories about the loss of a partner, one with a tragic twist but another is a love story which did not end with a wartime tragedy, but has an air of mystery and enduring affection.

A story by an 11 years old has hope as his theme, but describes a scenario that no child should experience, but sadly in the world today many children lose family to wartime conflict. He sets the story in his local area, in a street where he lives in Eltham, and shows a fortitude of spirit as he loses everything. You are left wondering - what happens next?

We have happy weddings at Eltham Palace and the 16c Tudor Barn and stories set in, the Tarn Park, the Eltham Centre library and St John's Church. Stories are funny and sad.

With a range of themes and emotions contained in so few words, these stories win our hearts and sometimes leave us wanting to know more.

A Letter To Pete
by Sue Head

Dear Pete

I found an old shoe-box of your letters written so many years ago. How long ago was it that I stood alone and forlorn on the platform at Eltham Park watching and waving your train goodbye? I remember it pulling away, the horn sounding and a plume of white steam being muffled as it disappeared under the Westmount Road arch. The train was carrying you and your folks on a mammoth journey to a new life in Australia.

That was over fifty-odd years ago, when I was fourteen and you fifteen. We were too young to be in love but it felt real and, for me, that feeing has never changed throughout the years. We promised we would write and that's what we did; for a while.

Eltham was never the same without you Pete. The park didn't look as green; the open air lido seemed empty and the water colder. Stopping to buy an ice cream cone at the swimming pool café was fun no more.

I can still see you waiting outside the fishmongers in Westmount Road on your bike; waiting for John. I remember us meeting at the cinema. The Palace was called the flea-pit for some reason so we used to go to the Gamount which was grander. Do you remember the youth club dances where we jived and danced? It was such an innocent and romantic time.

But you left for a new life and I stayed. We lost touch and memories fade. I'm not even sure you're still in Australia and I only have a long-ago address but when I found your letters today I wanted to write and to tell you that Eltham was never same without you.

Love from long ago - Sue

See you soon Stan
by David Culver

I had often wondered what I would find to do when I retired; in the event, the decision was made for me - I would learn how to walk again, after a stroke. At first, a gentle trip to the High Street, then, as my balance and confidence improved, the Park, the Pleasaunce, the Palace - further and further - Avery Hill and Sutcliffe Park.

On my walks, I occasionally saw an old man in even worse shape than me, apparently exercising in much the same way; one day, as we came face to face, I realised that we knew each other. As young men, finding our feet in civilian life after National Service, we had worked in the same small office building, and used the same pub. I had no idea that he lived in Eltham - was not even sure of his name; his boss (to whom he could be astonishingly rude) called him Stanley, though this could as easily have been a surname as a forename.

Nevertheless, I called him Stan, and he did not seem to mind. He was everything that I was not - self assured, optimistic, an enthusiastic gambler, and endowed with a talent for making the most ordinary incident sound hilariously funny. He had always been overweight - now, it was clearly a problem.

"You look well!"
- Don't give me that, Stan. I've had a stroke, you know. But how are you?

Instantly he dropped into the old raconteur mode; he had diabetes, kidney trouble, and was due to see a heart specialist again after a quadruple by-pass. And his account of his encounters with the NHS, unbelievably, had me helpless with laughter.

"Must rush; can't keep the consultant waiting. See you soon"
-Yes, see you soon Stan.

But I haven't seen him again.

T MINUS 20 MINUTES
by Pam Percy

At T minus 20: Hope picked up her rucksack, jumped off the 286, and crossed the High Street. Her mission: to get to the rendezvous, Eltham Palace.

T minus 15: she strolled in the sun along North Park eyeing the large comfortable houses: three cars in the drive, well kept gardens, expensive curtains.

T minus 12: Hope crossed Court Road into Tilt Yard Approach. She scanned her Green Chain guide... "hammer-beam roof"... "origin of the Order of Garter... "many extravagant jousting tournaments". Hmm.

T minus 10: she passed The Orchard and, for the hundredth time, recalled the lonely hearts ad.

Walking man (34) wltm walking woman. London. Box 2743.

"Jasper" had suggested they walk a short stretch of the Green Chain, from Eltham Palace to Beckenham. "Jasper" what sort of name was that? He would wear a red neckerchief (was that slightly risqué?) and Hope her red bracelet.

Oh God, she thought, I hope he's not one of those weather-beaten walking hardies. Please, please, please don't let him have a floppy hat, a knitted tank top, or one of those map wallets dangling on his chest.

T minus 5: she turned into the entrance of Eltham Palace, smiling at the wonderful brickwork, clipped gardens and the moat, glistening in the winter sunlight.

T minus 2: Hope reviewed her opening gambit: A bold "Hi, I'm Hope, walking woman"? Or a more circumspect "Are you Jasper?" Her steps carried her over the stone bridge, closer.

T minus 1: Hope slowed down. She had cold feet. Was this another blunder? She forced herself to breathe deeply, persuading herself that she had nothing to lose – except lonely pride.

She sensed someone behind her and turned. Blond. Bearded. Normal.

"Hello Hope. I'm Jasper."

T.

Let the jousting begin.

Let the jousting begin.

FISH

by Margaret Lewis

She looked out of the window and saw that the rain had stopped and the wind was easing. Just right for a trip out. She hadn't been out since Christmas Eve and, apart from the phone call from her son Alan in Sydney, she hadn't spoken to anyone in almost a week. He'd rung to ask her what she was going to do with the money he'd sent her, but she had no idea. Harry had been a good provider both in life and death, and her wardrobe, cupboards and freezer were well stocked.

She and Harry had never needed anyone else so now she had few friends. Perhaps that was why Alan had left home all those years ago and settled so far away. Still no use in thinking about that now, she thought, as she buttoned up her coat and collected her walking stick. She would need it even though it was only a short walk to get the bus to Eltham. Sitting on the bus she suddenly knew what her treat would be. She'd go to Marks and get something really special for dinner. Some fish – maybe salmon and a few prawns.

The High Street seemed busy and she was glad she hadn't worn that fiddly hearing aid. All that noise. The green crossing light had just finished flashing but the road looked empty so she decided to cross. Pausing slightly she thought a bit more about what vegetables to buy. Then looking up she saw the distressed look on the car drivers face and his mouth open in a silent shout.

An Accomplished Life Continued: Eltham Crematorium

by Alex Farrow

In silence, heads bowed, we make our way over to the far crook of the tranquil gardens until we reach the spot. A little out the way and maybe not the most groomed but she'd like that. Never one to make a fuss, she was always his rock, his light.

Memories still a little hard to break the years of abandonment from his eyes as he'd smiled across at me. The smile didn't comfort, it ripped me inside, knowing that I couldn't do anything but grip his hand tighter.

We stood over the patch of ground, I couldn't tell you how long. Time didn't really have a clasp on this small speck of the world, not for us.

We laid flowers, of course from her beautiful garden. Snowdrops and bluebells always reminded me of racing through Oxleas wood with them both on Saturday afternoons while mum worked. I led my Grandfather over to the bench and we huddle up to keep warm. It was hard being the stronger one, still so young. I pushed down a lump in my throat and laughed a little, a nervous laugh so I felt I should justify it. "Remember that Easter when I tried teaching her to break dance and she took it a little too literally? Actually breaking her arm! 3 days before she got it checked at hospital. I'll always feel guilt about that" His heartbreaking stare glimmered as he pulled my chin up "Never! Her love for you let her leave a world better than she found it. You, your mum and sister gave her appreciation in the beauty of each day; she had an accomplished life because of your love"

A lone figure now I stand there once more, laying bluebells. Each accomplishment, each breath they continue on with me.

Goodbye James
by Dana Wiffen

Nora Cope sat looking out of the window of her care home, waiting for family to come and take her for an afternoon.

Her mind wandered to her happy time living in Eltham, a smile slowly crept across her face as she remembered her teenage years before she had become ill.

At the start of the war around 1940 she had cycled one day to meet her boyfriend called James, on this occasion he was in full RAF uniform and he excitedly told her he was being deployed to fly Spitfires. She kissed him and said "Goodbye James" not long after this day she received news that he had been shot down over France.

As a tear ran down her face she was suddenly cheered to see a familiar car pull into the car park, it was her brother hopefully taking her to one of her favourite places in Eltham.

As her illness had got worse the day trips had been shortened to afternoon trips to ensure she returned in time for her medication.

She was cheered to hear that they were on their way to Eltham Palace, all too soon it was time to return, and not long into the journey it had become obvious that something was wrong with the car's steering and in heavy rain they pulled over to see what the problem was.

From nowhere a man in RAF uniform had offered to help and as the car steamed up inside Norah had rubbed at the window as if she had seen someone familiar, with the urgency of getting Norah back, his help was welcomed and the car was soon fixed.

As the man was thanked for his help, he nodded towards the car disappearing into the rain, Norah was heard to quietly say "Goodbye James"

Solo Sausages Again
by Barbara Scott

The sound of the bell broke rudely into her musings. It was her stop already – nearly missed it. Eltham High Street managed to look cheerful through the grey drizzle, due to the Christmas lights and the crowds of bustling shoppers.

Pearl dodged her way through the people to the entrance of Sainsbury's. This evening was going to be different. The wire basket with its sad little one person portions, would not make her feel judged by the customers with trolleys loaded so high that they were in danger of causing a major incident, if the pusher cornered recklessly round the aisles.

Tonight was Singles Night, and she had picked up her blue sticker at the entrance, and would be discreetly eyeing the other basket holders, trying to spot fellow sticker wearers. Pearl's basket was beginning to get heavy, along with her heart, as blue stickers were few and far between.

"Oh well, time to get the sausages and leave", she thought.

Having selected the plump, garlic laden ones (who would care about her smelly breath?) she turned round despondently. Suddenly, her basket was wrenched out of her hand by another basket passing at speed, causing the contents of both to fall to the floor with a clatter. Pearl, embarrassed, bent down quickly to gather up her shopping.

Her eyes were transfixed by a superb pair of tanned legs. They slid up past navy shorts, and a navy shirt, alas, minus a sticker, to a smiling face she recognised. It was her postman.

"I've been too shy to ask you out before", he said, "but I'm hoping that the blue sticker means you would like to come out for a drink with me"

Saying "Yes", Pearl furtively replaced the garlic laden sausages.

Football in the Park
by Sue Williamson

I had just become captain of the school football team when Dad announced we were moving to Eltham. I clearly remember being as angry as a jar of trapped wasps. Mum adopted the brisk no-nonsense approach and insisted I would soon make new friends. However I was far from convinced, especially as she made arrangements for me to 'play' with seven years old Andrew who had a heart condition and rarely went out. I was all of nine and outraged that my mother expected me to entertain some sickly little kid.

With a very bad grace I slunk next door to confront Andrew who was thin and pale with a haunted expression. He seemed the nearest thing to a blue human being as I had ever seen.

One day he said he would like to go to Avery Hill Park. Our progress was slow and I was not that patient. Andrew sat on a bench and I kicked a ball so he could try to kick it back to me. Andrew told me he was soon to have a big operation. He was scared and looked bluer than ever. I felt a twinge of conscience and pulled a tiny plastic footballer out of my pocket. Lying that it was my lucky mascot I pushed it into his hand.

At about this time my parents separated so I soon forgot about Andrew. I'm in my forties now. Last year my son contracted meningitis. I did think of Andrew then and how little I had understood. In the hospital the consultant came to speak to my wife and me. He took something out of his pocket, a small plastic footballer. 'Well, it helped me,' he said. 'It will help your son too'.

First Love
by Shaheen Westcombe

Sara walked past St. Mary's Centre and headed towards the Polish food shop. She missed the hot nibbles from back home. Here they are known as Bombay mix but the taste is different. After grabbing a packet of nutty nibbles, her next destination was Marks and Spencer. She wanted a present for her mother. A friend was going to Bangladesh and had offered to carry it.

She bought a woollen cardigan, just what her mother would like and went upstairs to treat herself to a cup of tea and cakes. Sara sat by the window, sipping the hot tea. She kept thinking of the past year. Here she was in London, studying at Avery Hill College and staying with her aunt in Eltham.

Sara missed Samir, her childhood sweetheart and first love. They were hoping to get married one day. Samir's parents moved to Dubai. He went with them and promised to return but she never heard from him again. Sara was devastated and wondered how Samir could disappear from her life.

Sara got up to leave. Someone was waiting for her seat. She looked up and it was Samir. Was she dreaming? He was frail and had a scar on his forehead. Samir looked at her and nearly dropped the tray. 'My prayers have been answered,' he cried and hugged her.

In Dubai, Samir was involved in a serious car accident. He had multiple injuries and was in a coma for days. It was a miracle that he survived. He had come to London for a medical checkup. Samir had tried desperately to contact Sara but her parents had moved and she had left Bangladesh.

No one can ever separate them now… Tears of joy rolled down their cheeks as they stepped out into Eltham High Street holding hands…

The Man with the Grey-Striped Shopping Bag

by Aylia Fox

Luke was only 18 and enrolled on a college course at the Eltham Centre because he didn't know what to do with his life.

His journey there took him from the High Street, through the library and to the college doors. Luke soon realised that one old man was in the library all the time. He always sat at the same corner table where the daily newspapers were laid out for public use. Sometimes he read, sometimes he slept and sometimes he rummaged round in his grey-striped shopping bag looking for something that clearly wasn't there.

One day Luke decided to do his homework in the library but couldn't summon up the enthusiasm to start. His studies were going badly and he was considering giving up.

"Cheer up son," Luke looked up and realised the man with the grey-striped shopping bag was addressing him.

"I was fighting in North Africa when I was your age and got this…" he unbuttoned his shirt to reveal a vicious scar. "I survived and so will you. Just live every day as if it's your last, and you'll be fine." Luke grinned, muttered "thanks mate", and left.

A couple of days later he walked past the library and saw a huddle of people and a policewoman. A green medical-style screen had been erected and as he got closer he saw the man's grey-striped shopping bag poking out from underneath. As he absorbed the sight, a funeral director pushed by him carrying a stretcher.

What the old man had said came rushing back. Suddenly Luke realised he was alive with a future limited only by his own ambition.

He didn't know the old man's name. It didn't matter. What mattered was that he was going to live life differently from now on.

BANG!
by Jasmine Alvis

The champagne bottle went bang! Conversations stopped and laughters began. A drenched Simon pulled out the diamond ring and said, "Happy Valentine's Day darling". Nina was startled as she looked over his shoulder at the white shadowy female figure floating across the room close to the wooden ceiling beams. It was holding a couple of books.

The waitress brought towels to help them dry up. Nina asked about the figure, but no one had seen it. "Why only me?" she said. "Maybe because you are special" replied Simon. She looked lovingly into his eyes as he slipped the ring onto her finger. "Yes I will" she said.

They enjoyed the lunch of butter grilled scallops with salad, chargrilled steak with vegetables and fries and pistachio and chocolate souffle by the original fireplace of the Tudor Barn. When Nina went to the washroom, the figure was there again standing in the narrow pathway. When she looked again it was gone.

Still smelling of champagne the couple took a stroll along the grounds of Pleasaunce. The bed of yellow crocuses looked romantic for Valentine's Day and promised the arrival of spring.

The wood carvings of squirrel and dragon looked beautiful in the windy sunshine as did the fountain and squirrel hut on the tree top. They meandered along shrubs, beeholes and picnic areas. A little girl aged between 2 and 3 years old ran towards a puddle and enjoyed splashing with her pink wellington boots despite her mother's "no" calls.

As they walked over the footbridge over the moat, Nina felt a bump and she was thrown into the water. When she looked up the shadowy figure was floating above the water smiling. Simon pulled Nina out of the water.

Nina exclaimed, "Can't the spirit of Edith Nesbit rest in peace?"

A Past Love

by Julie Bartley

Jennifer had lived in Eltham for most of her life. She loved the History of the area, the lush green woodland and plentiful parks and commons.

Here she was 45, divorced, feeling anxious and unsettled walking towards The Well Hall Pleasaunce. It had been a childhood haunt of her and her friends, and as they all grew into young adults, it became a place to go "courting" as her parents' generation had referred to dating.

She was due to meet an old past love named Richard, they had been friends at secondary school and eventually dated for a while. They were besotted with each other for a few years, before leaving school aged about 18, when they then seemed to move about in different social groups. Jennifer had been distraught when they drifted apart, but felt too proud to explain to him at the time.

Here she found herself over 30 years later waiting to meet him again, by the Tudor Barn. A friend was in contact with him by Facebook and had sort of engineered the meeting, which Richard had apparently been very enthusiastic about.

The purple and yellow crocuses were sprouting through the grass, a sign of spring and the colour that was yet to appear.

"Jen" she heard her name called in a very familiar soft, smooth voice. Her heart leapt. She turned around and smiled, instantly her anxiety lifted and her fear left her as she saw her familiar past love approaching her.

"Hello Rich" she replied…….

OFF-ROAD
by Tom Ryan

I knew halfway round it would be the last time I took Vincent up to Oxleas. His skin was grey and papery and his breathing was bad, like sucking on a harmonica. We stopped by each bench so he could read the inscriptions. When he looked up and smiled from the wheelchair, my eyes caught me surprise. I didn't want him to see the tears.

My uncle was known for being full of it. Way back, he'd told us how he and granddad rowed over to England when the ferry sank, how he'd played for Belfast Celtic when they beat United in a friendly, how he'd married Lily his first day back from Korea. None of that could be true, and now there wasn't much time to get the real story. "Vincent", I started, "I …" but his white hand went up. He grimaced, and croaked "let's get back, Danny boy".

We were a long way out, above the castle. When we reached the shortcut, the steep back path over the ruts and roots, I paused. Vincent took a sharp breath, and turned on that open expression he had, like my brother's; not like mine. "What d'you think, son? We'll have a go, eh?"

Though the chair wasn't built for it, we went off-road. The level sections were no harder than juddering a shopping trolley across a car park. The uphill was a struggle, but he was so light it was only steering was the problem. Almost back to the meadow, the front wheel jammed against a tree root and Vincent tumbled out. I swallowed my heart back down. "Jesus, I'm sorry. Are you hurt?" He was barely moving under his blanket.

When I rolled him over, I thought he might be crying, but he was grinning.

The Butterfly Garden
by Jane Chandley

The last Sunday in July: Friends of the Tarn were giving their annual summertime teaparty.

Tarn, a member, enjoyed these get-togethers. After greeting friends, she strolled around the lake, tossing food to the wildlife, and entered the Butterfly Garden, the arch decorated with butterfly-painted tiles.

The sunshine filtered through the trees, butterflies drifted among the flowers, a robin perched nearby and a blackbird sang.

She sat on the beach, soon dozing, dreaming that they were living in Kenya again during that drought-stricken year when they drove to Massi Mara.

Late in the afternoon, they approached a shallow, placid stream where she saw a Long-tailed Whydah pair, the male jumping up and down repeatedly to impress his mate. Tara wanted to film his display although John was eager to cross the stream and arrive home before dark.

"Let's go," he suggested, but she continued filming, pausing when she heard a sound that surprised her: rain in the distant hills, welcome after a prolonged drought. Would the parched soil absorb it quickly enough? Within minutes, what she had feared happened. With a roar, the once calm stream had turned into a torrent. Trees and animals tumbled down with the swirling water.

Footsteps on gravel woke Tara, the dream still vivid. John was standing beside her.

"I was dreaming about the flash flood. The water sounded real."

"It wasn't dream-water. Norman has just turned on the fountain. That's what woke you".

"Perhaps," she murmured, still drowsy.

Her husband kissed her lightly on the forehead, exactly where a butterfly had alighted earlier. They walked up Court Road, hand-in-hand, to their maisonette in Tarnwood Park, their first home in London, chosen because Mottingham Station was convenient, but mainly because they had strolled around The Tarn first. The beautiful park decided for them even before they had viewed the property. The scene from their window delighted them: a perfect view of The Tarn.

Marriage at the Barn

by James Byrnes - age 11

When I woke, I dashed downstairs. I saw everyone getting ready for my mum and dad's big day. As fast as I could, I had my breakfast so I could get ready too. When we were all finally ready, we got in the cars and we were on our way to the Tudor Barn. When we arrived everyone was seated and waiting with smiles all round. As the music started my brothers and I walked down the aisle, when we got to our seats I looked round at my beautiful mum walking down the aisle.

My mum and dad looked at each other and smiled with such love in their eyes, my mum looked as beautiful as a princess. As the registrar began to wed my mum and dad they started to say their vows, as my uncle gave my dad the wedding ring my mum was beaming with joy.

After they put the rings on each other the registrar said "you may now kiss the bride" as they kissed, everyone stood up and clapped. Next they went to sign the marriage book, everyone was so happy for them they were still clapping, unable to contain their happiness.

After they had both signed the marriage book it was time for pictures and the party! My mum and dad had booked an awesome entertainer for us, he did balloon models, I got a big hat and a super mouse it was so cool. Then we stopped for ten minutes because it was time for my mum and dad's dance. Their song was 'my best friend' by Tim Mc Graw. When their dance was over the entertainer took us outside for games. As one by one everyone left there was only us left, everyone loved it. I know I did!!!!

HOPE
by Melek Ibrahim - age 11

A chill ran down my spine, the evening breeze blew my hair behind me. I may have lost my home, my school and my happiness, but nothing would take the one thing I had left the one thing I could rely on: hope.

One hour ago

Walking out the door, I pulled my warm coat over my shoulders and wrapped my white scarf round my neck. I ran round the corner to the course. I went straight in to meet Laura. I looked around, she wasn't there.

"Have you seen Laura today", I asked

"No, sorry." Emily replied concentrating on her game of table football against Jake.

Bang! Just as I went to open it, I fell back and landed right under the door which had just flown of its hinges.

"Help! My arm!" I cried. Jake and Emily lifted the heavy weight off me. My arm moaned painfully.

Laura rushed in crying. I had never seen her like this before.

"Bombs, outside!"

She looked down, stunned at the sight of me on the floor, she ran to get the first aid kit.

In a couple of minutes, I was bandaged up and watching the bombs land on my school.

Destroyed, my home, my school. What about my family, my parents, little Nancy- so innocent.

The bombs stopped but fires kept burning and spreading from road to road.

We went outside and walked up to William Barefoot Drive where my house used to stand. I heard a scream, little girl's scream. Nancy's scream. I scurried through the ruins of what used to be called home. There was no sign of my parents. What if that scream was her last? What if it's too late? It's never too late I thought. Nancy lay still, motionless.

Rembember
by Ann Tolladay

When he and his brothers finished at Roper Street school, he felt such pride when he was taken on as an under gardener at Eltham Palace. Bill was working in the post office in Passey Place and Eddy worked in the bank at the cross roads.

On a Friday they would meet up for a pint or two at the Greyhound pub. One night it was so crowded they went round the corner to The Rising Sun and there she was, fate had put the love of his life in front of him, all blond hair and blue eyes. They got talking and to his surprise she agreed to met him the next afternoon.

The Tarn could not have looked better, sun lush greens and flowers. Their feelings for each other blossomed too, they married at St. Johns Church and a year later the twins were born. They lived very contently in a two up two down in Sun Yard. Money was short, but his wife and children gave him a life full of love.

Now he lay here in the mud soaking wet cold and yes angry. The anger welled up in him, the destruction and carnage they were causing must be stopped. It was for the love of what he had left behind, for little families like his that he was prepared to do this terrible thing. The whistle sounded then the movement of men going over the top like a great unstoppable wave. At that moment he knew that what ever his fate, in one part of London what he had planted would continue to grow and even in a hundred years time people would remember and be proud of the sacrifice they were making.

Dress Code: Poirot
by Karen Storey

Propelled by your derision, the invitation skids across the kitchen table. Dress Code: Poirot - ridiculous, you say. But to me it's perfect. Like Sam and Alex, I adore the 1930s, and immediately imagine myself at their wedding in a floral frock from that intriguing little vintage shop just off the High Street.

On the day, I manage to coax you into a sharp double-breasted suit and trilby, but not out of your sulks. The taxi driver's prattle fills the silence that gapes between us as we drive up to the imposing entrance of Eltham Palace. Stepping out of the cab, I'm thankful to be swallowed up by the throng of twittering guests, bright in their celebratory plumage; only you and your monosyllables resist the joyous atmosphere.

Inside, I exclaim at the elegance and unexpected familiarity of the Art Deco marquetry and the glazed dome above us, but your only response is a grumble that I watch too many period dramas. When we stand for the entrance of the bridal couple, I glance at your forbidding profile and in that moment I see the stranger you have become. As vows are exchanged, my tears celebrate one relationship and mourn another. But when Sam and Alex turn to their guests, I forget my heartache as their smiles dazzle beneath their matching waxed moustaches.

1907 - King John's Palace - Eltham

1917 - Eltham High Street - Eltham

MEMORIES

Eltham is a place full of memories. With a royal history of kings and knights, it was of no surprise that Eltham Palace inspired a number of stories, some with strange meetings across the centuries. There is also a story set in 1651 and a story describing the grave in St John's Church of an aborigine brought to Eltham from Australia in the 18th century.

Stories were full of personal memories, finding family wartime papers, coming to an Eltham school from Jamaica, watching the Last Eltham Tram in 1952, the dance hall above Burtons menswear shop, the swimming pool, preparing for a solo, or the dread of the polio jab. School days and teenage years were remembered, and other stories recall funny and happy incidents which make up everyday life. One story is written from the viewpoint of an Eltham road, reminding us of the many feet and vehicles which have passed this way.

The range of memories which inspired our stories stretch back hundreds of years and are an important aspect of creativity in Eltham.

LAST RIDE ON 'THE ELTHAM FLYER' 5TH JULY 1952

by Ernest Jupp

'Please Dad - it's our last chance to ride on a tram!', pleaded Derek Skinner, aged 11.
'I don't know what all the fuss is about - I'll be glad tomorrow when the buses take over'.
'But Dad', it's historic', he tried.
'Hysteric more like, and you've Sunday school in the morning.'
'But I want a ride on London's very last tram - it's a 38 from Woolwich'.
'Woolwich? - not likely!'
Derek changed tack.
'Can we catch the last 46 tram from Eltham Church then?', he asked. 'We can walk there in 5 minutes'.
'OK, but it won't be London's very last tram will it?'
Accepting this, Derek said, 'Thanks Dad', with scant enthusiasm.

Thus, at the appointed hour, Skinner and son waited outside Burton's, opposite Eltham Church. After a long gap between trams, what surely must be the last number 46 came swaying into view up the hill from Well Hall like a lighted galleon. Someone had chalked up 'The Eltham Flyer' on the front, and although it was plainly full, the kindly conductor, in party mood, helped them aboard. Even Mr Skinner was infected with the jolly atmosphere, and said to Derek 'We'll stay on to New Cross if you like'. Derek liked!

However, progress was so incredibly slow through enormous crowds at 'The Yorkshire Grey', Lee Green and Lewisham that they were over an hour late at New Cross, and as the tramcar ground noisily to a halt outside the depot, which had seemed deserted, an irate Inspector ran up shouting, 'Do you lot realise you've come in half an hour after the official last tram?' *

'Blimey', exclaimed Skinner senior, 'We were on London's last tram after all'.
'Thanks Dad', said Derek meaningfully, placing their tickets safely in his pocket.
'Er, Dad, how are we getting home?'.
'Blowed if I know!'.

* The 46 tram from Eltham really did arrive at New Cross depot just as described, at about 1.45am, about 30 minutes after 'London's last tram', and well after an impressive ceremony had concluded!

A Warm Welcome to Coldharbour
by Dawn Winchester

"Keep polishing!" encouraged my Mum, brightly. "It will keep us warm."
There we were, on our hands and knees, polishing the bare, black floor in the hallway. It didn't need polishing but it was February 1953 – and a particularly cold one at that. After all, we had moved to Coldharbour!

Two months before my third birthday and just Mum, Dad and me in our own flat. No more being squashed into Grandma and Granddad's back bedroom together. What more could we want? I even had a room to myself which Jack Frost visited every night to draw beautiful patterns on the inside of the Crittall windows.

We quickly got to know the family living in the flat directly underneath ours. No sooner had we got the open fire burning nicely in the living room grate, when there was a knock on the open door.

The welcoming man introduced himself as our downstairs neighbour but seemed anxious as he asked whether we had ignited our fire. Although they had not yet lit their own, a furnace was raging fiercely in their grate downstairs and he suspected that our shared chimney was ablaze!

Sure enough, smoke and flames were billowing from the top of the chimney outside and from deep inside the chimney breast came an ominous rumbling and roaring. The Chief Fireman enlisted my help by putting his white helmet on my head. While I struggled to peer beneath it and prevent my legs from buckling under the weight, he and his firefighters soon had the situation under control.

So, this was our beginning on Coldharbour Estate but there was much more to come. A momentous event was occurring in June and the neighbours were getting together to celebrate the beginning of the New Elizabethan age ………. but that's another story.

ONE HIT WONDER
by Sarah Smith

We were walking along with the others through the High Street after dinner. "My greatest moment was a date with a pop star", he said. "Get you!" I smiled.

"It was 1964 and I was at a college in London training to be a lawyer. My father was a Doctor and I always knew that a profession was the thing to have. I was part of a committee that organised entertainment, things like parties, balls and bands." I remembered my own student days in the 1980's. The scruffy boys in leather jackets and grubby girls who looked like they had just got out of bed ran the "Ents". Their desks were littered with beer cans and fag ends.

"Gina Jay was a one hit wonder we'd booked. She was tiny. Like a little ballerina with a big blond hair-do and huge eyes. After the gig I thanked her for playing and nervously asked if she wanted to come to a party. I expected a brush off but instead she looked up, smiled and said that she would love to.

We listened to records on the Dansette. I drank beer and she drank Martini. I wasn't a great talker and after the first pint she put her arms around my neck to dance and we shuffled on a worn carpet. Afterwards I walked her to the place she was staying. We stood on the step and I bent down and kissed her."

"What happened next?" I asked, expecting more. "Oh, nothing. I went back to the party, I suppose, and she went onto the next gig. Her pop career fizzled out and that was that."

A Minor Success

by Geoff Lander

Sammy was one of those children of whom little is expected. Fittingly, he was looking up towards the Palace now, dreaming. Sammy was dreaming. He watched the autumn leaves flutter by and wondered, well, very little. He might have wondered if yellow leaves fluttered like this in Henry VIII's time but he didn't because, because he was Sammy.

He quite liked the music lesson. In the future he would become a capable drummer and guitarist but now he was dreaming. He wasn't dreaming maliciously, it just was in his gentle nature.

Mr Crump was irritable today. He wasn't often irritable. He was, in fact, positively irascible but Sammy didn't know and would probably never know what irascible means.

Tlong!

Sammy awoke. With a sickening clonk Mr. Crump had, well, crumpled. His head had hit the tiles, big time. A little trickle of blood came from Mr. Crump's head. Some of the cleverer girls wept. Others, boys and girls looked on in horrified amazement.

Sammy, however, was off. He didn't run. No running in the corridors! He knew exactly where the office was. He forgot to knock. The secretary looked up.

"Yes Sammy? Why aren't you in class? And it's polite to..."

"Mr. Crump's fallen over. He's not moving Miss. His head is bleeding."

Mrs. Patel was up in a flash. "Oh dear! He's probably forgotten his medication again."

Forgetting was a sin, Sammy had already mastered it. He understood and yet he didn't.

"Well done, Sammy. Good boy."

Sammy was one of those children of whom little is expected but now he had an odd feeling, albeit briefly and for the first time in his life he had had a minor success. In an Eltham classroom, Sammy, yes, you know Dreamy Sammy, Dreamy Sammy had showed some initiative.

Our Dream Home
by Elisabetta Pancucci

They held hands. He let her hold the key. She'd waited years for this. Together they walked through the gates. The rain-soaked January had left the path shimmering in the dark. The rose bushes stood to attention in their rows, pruned to half their usual height. In a few months they would be in their full glory, their blooms filling the air with sweetness.

The door opened with a click. The warmth greeted them. He walked in to the living room. She went to the kitchen.

"It's got an Art Deco fireplace! We can sit either side of it and warm our toes on cold, frosty nights!" He cried.

He stroked the mantelpiece, grinning from ear to ear.

"I can see the garden from the kitchen sink." She called. "There are fox cubs playing out there! There's a moat too!"

They met in the Great Hall and ran up the stairs, giggling like excited children. Their faces gleamed in the twilight, their smiles shone like the moonlight.

"A roll top bath! I'll put candles all around and listen to the radio", She whispered. He smiled and pulled her close to him as they entered the bedroom.

They switched on the bedside lamps. As she drew the curtains closed she was reminded of her grandmother's gravestone on which the inscription read: 'Draw the curtains and light the lamps, and be, from the dark night, withdrawn together.'

They lay side by side, hand in hand on top of the velveteen eiderdown, carefully slipping off their shoes. Curling their toes they closed their eyes.

He spoke out into the amber-lit room, "Listen to that."

"I can't hear anything". She answered.

"Peace at last."

They rolled over to face one another and opened their eyes.

"We found it! Our Palace!"

Then they kissed.

A Royal Encounter
by Jill Lee

I was passing the gates of Eltham Palace one day when I noticed a heavy police presence. I paused in time to see Prince Charles coming out flanked by his security guards.

He must have remembered seeing me in the Mall on Coronation Day because he approached me and said, "Do you live round here?"

I said that I did and he then asked if I sat in the Palace grounds in the evenings. I explained that they were not open at that time but that my garden was situated on the site of the original Palace kitchen garden and I did sit there.

He said he enjoyed sitting in his garden at Highgrove and hoped that I would visit it. He then proceeded to walk to his car where he sat in the back seat, removed a comb from his pocket and combed his hair.

Not many people have seen him do that!

My Soul Still Rests at Eltham Palace

by Anne Sharman

The fragrance from the beautiful roses in the sunken garden gave off a heady perfume. It was a scorching hot day and shielding my eyes from the bright sun with my hand, I took in the beauty of Eltham Palace. How glad I was to have made contact again with the Courtaulds, fancy bumping into them at Claridge's after such a long time. It was so generous of them to invite me to spend some time here in Eltham with them.

Everyone else was taking an afternoon nap but it was too hot and I was too interested in exploring the rest of the grounds. Wandering around I was intrigued to stumble upon a place that was surrounded with yew bushes and hidden away from the rest of the house and gardens. Even more exciting it revealed a secluded swimming pool! How wonderful! It was meltingly hot and the water looked cool, clear and so inviting, I was so tempted to strip off and dive in! Why not I thought?

Looking around I could see no one else was in sight and impulsively I stripped down to my petticoat and dived into the cool clear water. Unfortunately, the water was much shallower than I had anticipated. My breath was forced out of me with the shock, a streak of red spiralled out in front of me turning the water pink. I began to float effortlessly upwards towards the golden sunlight that called to me through the ripples on the surface of the water.

My soul still rests at Eltham Palace, down by the yew bushes where the pool used to be. Sometimes, on a hot summer's day you will see me there if you look close enough. I cannot leave it is my home.

A Tale from Eltham Green Comprehensive School

by Shirley Fox

As the only black pupil from Jamaica in the newly opened Eltham Green Comprehensive School for 2000 pupils in September 1956, I was overwhelmed by its size, the English accents of my fellow pupils and teachers, and the general culture of my newly adopted country. I was thrown in the deep end, immediately facing 'O' levels in subjects that were largely culture biased. Studying 'Pride and Prejudice' by Jane Austen was a case in point. How could I relate to a novel deeply rooted in the society of English landed gentry, when I had grown up in a country village in Jamaica? The 'Agrarian Revolution' in History was equally alien. Thankfully, other subjects were familiar from my earlier education.

When children asked about my life in trees or wearing feathers, I had no idea what they were talking about. Judy, a friend, tried to protect me from pupils' curiosity about a black girl thrown into their midst. The teachers also misinterpreted my frequent nervous giggling and tendency to bury my face in the desk, as being rude, so I spent many occasions in the corridor. By the second year at Eltham Green I had gained the respect of several teachers, because, against all odds, I had successfully passed six 'O' level subjects. I was made a junior prefect in the lower sixth form and a school prefect in the upper.

Fond memories linger of friendships formed, teachers who understood and helped me greatly, and the honour of receiving my examination certificate from John Hunt (of Everest fame). I still treasure my book of autographs from both pupils and teachers when leaving school. My motto remains, as one teacher inscribed, "Live as if you...die tomorrow, Learn as if you...live forever!"

Eltham Green – "Unforgettable, Unforgotten!"

From Pantomime to Poltergeist
by Paul Cookson

It may seem unlikely but I was painting pantomime scenery amid the dusty organ pipes of Eltham's Christchurch choir loft.

I had volunteered to paint the backdrops for a Priory Players Pantomime. What I had not been told was that I could not use the stage until the week before the first performance. I had to find somewhere else to work on the backdrops.

The solution turned out to be the long back wall of the church choir loft. My father was choir master, so permission and access would be no problem. Fortuitously, a water pipe ran at high level along the back wall for attaching the backdrops.

Time was short so I started work straight away. On that particular Saturday afternoon time was definitely running out. As I painted, the light was beginning to fade, leaving only the dim fluorescent choir light. The church below was now in darkness and I needed some fresh water. I descended to the blackness of the church, and made my uncertain way to the sacristy. Although familiar with the church, I was surprised how uneasy I felt. I retraced my steps away from the comforting light of the sacristy and once more became absorbed in my painting.

It was approaching midnight when I heard the noise….a slow menacing shuffle mounting the choir steps. My mouth became dry and my heart raced. I saw a white haired spectral figure, with flowing white robes, emerging from the gloom. It spoke.

"Paul! What are you doing working at this time of night?"

It was old Fr. Ambrose. His Priory bedroom was on the other side of the choir loft wall. He had heard strange noises emanating from the church and had bravely come, in his nightshirt, to investigate. He was not amused but we were both relieved.

Last Swim
by Jill Carr

Janet had been to the lido many times before. In fact she had practically lived there every summer holiday while at secondary school. Each morning she would make a packed lunch, gather her swimming gear and go off to meet her friends. All day was spent sitting or lying on the sun terrace. On a hot day it was packed, with barely enough space to lay out her towel. To join the long queue snaking from the hatch of the cafe she would have to carefully pick her way through the patchwork of towels, some with an outstretched body on others marking the territory 'til the owner returned from a dip in the cool water or their place in the cafe queue. Her and her friends had their own favourite spot up the steps and to the left of the fountain (the opposite side to the cafes snake). Easy to acquire on the cooler days, but not so when the sun shore warm and bright. Then the people of Eltham and the surrounding areas came out in force.

This afternoon was different. It was a lovely warm day but the schools were yet to break up, so the lido was practically empty.

Janet worked in a shop in the high street and Thursday was half day closing. The perfect chance for a dip. Her mum had decided to join her. That hadn't happened since the days of her early childhood when she couldn't swim and even the shallow end was too deep to stand. As they approached the familiar board stood outside with the pool information and the current temperature of the water (never very warm). The turnstile in the narrow entrance and the face of the lady taking the money were so familiar. Likewise the changing rooms down either side and the lady handing you a wire basket to put your clothes in to be safely stored on a shelf for the duration of your visit.

Ted's Journey
by Luke Edeson

Trains screeching, horns blasting, pedestrians marching; Ted was used to the pace of life in the London suburbs. He visited the Kent countryside once and was immediately deafened by the silence.

Recently however, he'd noticed that the trains weren't running as regularly as they used to. At first he wasn't sure they had changed at all, no one else seemed to notice, but as the days and weeks slipped by, it became clear.

Fewer and fewer commuters packed the now infrequent trains; the platforms were a no man's land of serenity. Something was happening.

The cars also began to slow down, their glistening bodywork taking on a duller, more humble tone.

Pedestrians that had once scrambled down Southwood Road, desperate to pierce the heart of London, now walked. The stress etched in their faces had been erased and replaced by smiles and laughter. Life was changing, slowing down.

Channels disappeared on Ted's television. No-one had a mobile phone or even spoke about the internet. Then it struck him like the crack of a gun: he was travelling through time.

Excitement and fear raced through Ted's veins. He was alone on the most fantastic, frightening ride of his life. He rode the wave of euphoria. But it didn't last long. The atmosphere around the town changed. Joy had invaded the community, bunting engulfed SE9. Every street became a sea of trestle tables, overloaded with sandwiches and pastries - celebration.

A strange celebration for hidden behind a façade of joy, relief and happiness, was pain. Ted had no idea what had caused this pain.

The next day, wandering aimlessly along Green Lane, he knew.

Standing still, frozen by the scream of the engine above him, he watched as the last German bomb to be dropped on London fell silently to the ground.

Yours Faithfully, Eltham
by Alex Wingham

When I wake up in the morning it can be hard. Not always, just sometimes. Sundays are easier, less people walking over me. Monday can be tough. 8.30pm, the school run, the lates for work and the just coming home crowd. I mean I don't mind, that's what I am here for, all sorts of people. "The Good, the Bad and the Ugly", makes no difference to me.

Now days it is all about the town planning, the changes they want can be hard. The weight on my shoulders came with the Progress Estate and the noise with the A2. Every day however I do say a little prayer saying "thank you for leaving the parks" over and over again. I mean I am not as young as I used to be. I don't want to grumble but I do look back to the days of the horse and carriage and think those were the days, but the cars kept coming. Sometimes I can hardly breathe from the fumes but only if the weather is heavy. It's not all bad. The smell from Costa in the morning can make a bad day better and don't even start me on the smells from the bakery.

Most days it's the same, same people, same day, same thing. Although every little while a surprise visitor comes and everyone gets excited, I love it when that happens. Who wouldn't? I mean Kings and Queens, Bob and Kate, even Jude Law (he was always my favourite). Days like those are the reasons for staying.

Anyway enough of me going on; I better get back or they would put another stupid roundabout in without thinking about it. Don't get me wrong I love being me but sometimes, just sometimes on that busy Monday morning I wish everyone would go to New Eltham and give me the day off.

THE RICH SCOUNDREL
by Teresa Nash

It is the year of Our Lord 1651; and I, John Piper of this parish of Eltham, have just been to show fealty to the new Lord, the villain Nathaniel Rich. We are told that if we are lucky, he may give us employment in the village. I went for the sake of my mother and sisters, for now that I am the man of the house, I need to bring in a wage. It was all I could do to stop myself from spitting in his face and I sometimes wonder if he will be murdered in his bed, such is the hate felt for him in this parish.

But such heroics are not for the folk of this village for we are just boys and old timers left to care for the women and the farms. For all in Eltham loved our King and our brave men went gladly to fight by his side against the traitor Cromwell and many valiantly gave their lives as did, eventually, our noble King himself.

It was while they were away so fighting that Rich's men came to our village. They said we were sinners to keep such an audacious palace and treasures in the church. They stripped our church of its treasures. The pulled down the palace fences and slaughtered the deer. Not a tree did they leave standing. Then Rich came to inspect their handy work although he told us he had come to stop them but oh too late.

Our beloved village now worthless, Rich has bought the palace for a song. We have little choice here but to pay homage and hope for work. But the man is a scoundrel and woe betide him when he faces our Lord on Judgement Day.

A Link to Eltham's Past

by Spencer Drury

My mother said "I was clearing the garage and came across your father's old stuff. Do you want to take a look?"

My father died when I was eleven, so a chance to delve into his past was an exciting opportunity. The 'stuff' was six solid, dark brown, wicker chests each with an aged, green canvas cover with the word 'Saddlers' stamped on it.

"They were carried round Burma when he was in the Indian Army" my mother commented. I knew he served with General Slim's 'Forgotten Army' and spoke Urdu but hadn't realised he was in the Indian Army.

The baskets creaked as I opened them, revealing army uniforms, a tattered Union Jack, maps of India and a range of veterinary tools.

Most amazing of all was a folded map on crisp, delicate, slightly yellowed paper. The top right corner was crumpled but as I opened it I recognised my father's name in his neat, precise handwriting. The 'K.Drury' was slightly smudged but above it was printed the words:-

No 3 Platoon Area – 'A' company
21st County of London Battalion
HOME GUARD

The map was dated July 1942.

As I unfolded the rest, I recognised places I know well – among them Oxleas Wood; Eltham Park North and Crookston Road. There were less familiar features like the Falconwood Hotel; BB (with barrage balloons drawn alongside) and the orchard where Kenilworth Gardens now stands.

The map was of Eltham - not just where my family and I live, but also where I am a Councillor. I knew my father was raised in Eltham, but didn't realise that he had served here prior to going to India. It was an amazing, pleasurable shock; finding this tangled thread reaching from my family's past and Eltham's history all the way to the present.

Queenscroft Park 1980

by Sheila Bishop

The sun still finding her place as I hurried along Kingsground, I had been to this park so many times, but today was different today was special. The gate already open and the gardeners busy. I stood at the top of the path and looked down towards the hut. It sat back from the small bridge and looked over the paddling pool.

The Magpies and crows strutted their stuff and greeted me with their usual loud cries, squirrels bounced across the path as if trying to remember where they'd left things. Taking a deep breath I walked down past the drinking fountain and into the hut, I was handed my overall and a badge on which was written; 'We Govern by Serving', I smiled, I liked that, respect on both sides.

The Sun fully awake and as eager as the trickle of small children that seemed to appear as if by magic, carrying towels and sandwiches, sun warmed drinks, balls and rings.

I was given a whistle and a few instructions and my first day as a park attendant began.

I rubbed suntan lotion on small shoulders, minded packed lunches, handed out toilet paper, stuck on plasters and shouted, "No dogs and get off your bike." We picked up litter and cleaned toilets, kept the older kids off the swings and out the pool (sorry but under twelves only). We did our best to keep them all safe and let them have fun.

Queenscroft Park with its boating lake, paddling pool, swings, skating ring, tuck shop and magic shows. All made for magical carefree days that ended when the sky lost its grip on the sun as she cast dappled fingerprints on the now still pool. The bell was rung and the gates locked.

The Solo
by Linda D'amiral

"Nell, she's got the solo", preened my mother, as she patted the huge beehive hairdo that sat proudly on top of her head.

"Well it's a ballet dress, one of those longer ones, I'll put her on".

The receiver was handed to me and I began to explain to my mum's sister the costume I needed for my performance at the Woolwich Town Hall. It was one of several outfits that had to be made in just a couple of weeks for a selection of tap, modern and ballet dances that I was to perform as a member of the Sybil Ansell School of Theatre Dance.

Every Saturday morning after I had purchased a large twist at Ayer's the Bakers, for dad's tea, I made my way along to the school that was situated above Burtons (now Macdonalds). Sometimes I would stop and glance at the photos that were displayed in the doorway of past performances then climb the stairs, up past the billiard hall and on to the top floor.

There was always a buzz of activity as I pulled open the door. Mums collecting daughters, children changing shoes, the pianist shuffling music sheets and there in the middle of it all, Sybil, in her silver t-strap dance shoes. She was my idol the one that I aspired to. I had worked so hard and never missed a lesson and now I had been chosen to perform a solo.

Finally the night arrived and I was waiting in the wings, dressed in my beautiful blue dress compliments of Aunt Nell. I took my place in the centre of the stage and froze. I looked beyond the footlights and there shone the "beehive", and my feet took flight.

Thanks Mum, my true inspiration.

Terror in Eltham, 1959
by Chris Almond

It was a bright morning when I awoke all those years ago, but my spirits were not lifted by the sunshine, for this was a day of dread. Normally I would be going to Eltham Church of England Primary School, where Miss Sexton would do her best to make a scholar out of me. Today however, I had to make a much darker journey. "Time to go" said Mum sternly, as I tried to find any excuse to delay our departure.

We left our home in Glenhouse Road and went on foot down Glenlea Road, across Well Hall Road and into Sherard Road. Usually I would stop to watch the engine shunting coal trucks in the sidings, but I was too preoccupied with impending terror to pay much attention. We turned into Prince John Road and then Keynsham Road, by which time my heart was pounding and I had butterflies in my stomach. "Not far to go now" said Mum menacingly. I knew just how those French aristocrats felt in the tumbrels, en route for their rendezvous with Madame Guillotine. We made one final turn and there just ahead was Destination Doom – sometimes called the Lionel Road Clinic.

Sweat was pouring down my brow, as we checked in and I waited my turn to be summoned to the torture chamber. Suddenly it was time. "This may hurt a little" said the nurse with a malevolent grin. I turned away and gritted my teeth, as a large needle hovered near my shoulder. There was a moment of exquisite pain and then it was all over. I turned back to find a saucer of sweets being thrust towards me. "You won't die from polio now" said the nurse reassuringly. Miss Sexton might yet have a scholar, but hardly a hero.

My Mispent Youth
by Mick Cohen

Un…be…lie…va…ble!!!!!!!!!!!

It was still standing! The portal! The gateway to memories of my schooldays!
I stood and gazed for several moments at the edifice before me. Should I go in? Would my memories be shattered?

I opened the glass door and stepped in. Wow! There had been a make-over, as gone were the plastic covered seats and the sticky floor…… yet, it was still the same. This was the WIMPY BAR! Eltham's Mecca of fast food; a schoolboy's Nirvana!

I sat down at a table and picked up the laminated menu and the memories came flooding back.

Racing out of school to catch the bus to Eltham High Street. This was the Swinging Sixties – destination WIMPY!! Bounding up the stairs on the bus to the top deck, where boys lit up illegal smokes, with the bravado of youth and the cough of the unfamiliar! Downstairs we hung from the bar on the bus' platform, daring each other who could hang out the furthest! Waving at the girls from local schools and calling out their names. "Susan James," (whatever happened to her?) "Lesley Behan." (who could give their daughter a name like that?) It was only years later I realised the terrible faux-pas her parents had made.

Arriving at the Wimpy Bar, pushing and barging each other to grab the best seat! Ordering was simple …………

"What can I get you Sir?" A voice broke into my reverie, bringing me back to the present. There was - there is - there always will be – only one reply. "Bender and chips, please!"

The Bender! The Michelin star of fast-food! A frankfurter sausage, so cleverly cut, it could bend round half a tomato on a bun. What more could a boy ask for?!

So I sat there, with my memories, and a Wimpy Bender! Result …. Happiness!!!

In Some Corner of a Foreign Field
by Luke Carter

The church of St John the Baptist soars brilliantly. Its bells ring out shrill and purposeful and the sound fights to be heard among cars and people and ringtones.

Yet wrapped quietly in crumbling brick, hidden between high rise flats and hectic highways, sits its unimposing graveyard. It is a noiseless place, even though it should not be. It is as if the lichen heavy headstones are absorbing the sound; as if even the street noise knows to be respectful.

Within the walls, granite and marble and stone compete for space and affection. Flowers lay on some, graffiti on others. The grass grows uninterrupted on damp earth. Spleenwort and Spring-Beauty emerge from the cracked pavement. And all is overlooked by the ancient Yew, tough and rugged. It is not forgotten, only overlooked.

In its most eastern corner, tucked tightly against the walled perimeter, is a story that is just that. Its headstone reads,

In Memory of Yemmerrawanyea
A Native of NEW SOUTH WALES
Who died the 18th of May 1794

Yemmerrawanyea was one of the first Australian aborigines brought to England. He was a small sensation of his day, paraded as a curiosity. He was housed in Mayfair, introduced to Kings, visited parliament, St Pauls and the theatre. He was educated to read and write, was dressed in fine suits and encouraged to share his customs-a medium between the unimaginably different worlds.

Yet he died just two years later, a supposed lung infection, brought on by the damp. He had moved to Eltham prior for the fresher air and he was buried there too. He is tucked tightly against the walled perimeter. He was 19 years of age. His story is brave and bizarre. His name was Yemmerrawanyea and is hopefully one you will not overlook.

We Used to go Dancing at Burtons
by Chris Page

Marilyn, Jean, Linda and I, four Plumstead girls. In the year of our 'O' levels, we first ventured over to Eltham.

On the corner of the High Street, where McDonalds is now, was a branch of Montague Burton, the tailor. The stairs at the side led up to - 1st floor a Snooker Hall, 2nd floor a Dance Hall complete with mirrored ball and spot lights. Chairs were provided around the edge of the dance floor, but who wanted to sit down? We were there to dance. Well, jive actually as this was the pre Beatles era and our music was mostly Rock'nRoll. Elvis, Little Richard, Buddy Holly etcetera.

Saturday evenings would find us tripping up the stairs on our stilettos, ponytails bobbing, skirts with layers of net petticoats swinging. We would tap our toes to the beat, nonchalantly chatting, but all the time sizing up the prospective partners. No dancing together round our handbags in those days. The boys would all be in smart suits and winkle-pickers. No denim jeans. They were for work. Someone would stroll up and ask us to dance, sometimes without uttering a single word. A polite gesture was enough. If he was good looking that was a bonus. If not, well at least we had been asked. At the end of the evening we would compare notes, unless of course we were escorted home. Very romantic.

I met my first proper boyfriend there as the 50s became the 60s. Over 6 ft tall, slim with fair wavy hair, Frank was a local boy. Three years older than me and really quite good looking. We went 'steady for over a year and sometimes all these years later when I pass McDonalds I recall the happy times we spent together.

Palace Prediction
by Mark Wall

The discovery was beneath the haunted Eltham Palace. There on the walls of long rumoured but forgotten tunnels was the inscription; Apud DCC unde post diluvium, et tempestate, sol et coniungere luna, et faciet vindictam fortis. Vestibulum non nisi in perniciem suam interclusi, translated read; "In 700 hence, after storm and flood, the Sun will join the Moon and bring forth an avenging warrior. His path of destruction can only be stopped by the Key". Dated 1314, it carried the crest of Edward II.

While scholars debated, the rumours started that 700 hence meant 2014, and we were experiencing the storms and floods predicted, and in October 2014 a Solar eclipse would be the Sun and Moon joining.

Aided by web based conspiracy and doomsday theorists the news of the discovery went viral and was the talking point on every radio and television station, as well as at dinner parties or in casual conversation.

But what was the key?

To mention it was to conclude that the event could be stopped or averted.

The answer came quickly when another tunnel was discovered leading out of the palace grounds toward the Eltham town centre. There, a large key was found and just beyond, down a smaller tunnel was a solid wood and iron door.

Beyond the door, drinking artefacts and empty 'Key Ale' casks were strewn around a large cavern room which was beneath the Greyhound Inn. In the centre of the room was a long table and on it the original plans and drawings of the palace and tunnels.

Inspection of the plans revealed a small footnote in Latin, a startling revelation. Its translation read; "This night past, midst much merriment and drinking, we do joke as we have placed a spirituous inscription for the future to ponder".

Health and Safety
by Hugo Robinson - age 11

I stood beside the ruined palace walls, studying the roof of the great hall. The sun came out, dazzling my eyes. Taking a step backwards, I fell into an uncovered manhole, dropped about ten feet and landed in cold water. Splashing around, spluttering for breath, my flailing arms found an iron staple in the wall. I grabbed it, calmed myself, and climbed up to the top, popping out of a well in a large courtyard.

As I wrung out my wet clothes in the bright sunlight, I had an uneasy feeling. Suddenly two burly men in chain mail seized me roughly, demanding to know why I was there. "What do you mean?" I replied, "I'm an English Heritage member". I showed them my membership card assuming they were doing a re-enactment.

They gazed at the card in confusion. "A fool!" said one in disgust, "throw him out!" said the other. They pulled me across the moat bridge and pushed me out through the gate. "Hang on," I shouted, "what is this place? What year is it?" They stared at me.

"Eltham Palace!" said the tall one looking astonished, "the year of our Lord 1536. And you're lucky King Henry didn't see you!" Slamming the gate, they crossed back over the bridge leaving me nearly 500 years back in time.

I wanted to get back to the well. Creeping around the wall I found some ivy, clambered up and looked around. All was clear so I leapt down and ran towards the well. Half way there a large man in a crown appeared and standing between me and the well shouted "Halt there knave! Where art thou going?" I pushed him into the moat. He landed with an almighty splash scattering the alarmed ducks. He stood up, crowned with duckweed, spluttering with rage.

I leapt into the well. A strong arm hauled me up. I thought I had been captured but found myself staring at an English Heritage workman. "Wot did you fink you was doin', eh? It's dangerous down there. Who knows where that might lead."

My Life in Eltham
by Maureen Sanderson

...during the war.

I was born and grew up in Eltham living on the Middle Park Estate, I remember the war, it was just part of life. A doodle bug fell at the back of Middle Park School, luckily all the children were down the shelters, there was a huge bang and dirt and dust came down on us. All the mums rushed up to get their children who were very frightened, we then had to go to Kingspark School, where one day on the way home a stray German plane opened fire on the children, people came out of their houses and gathered children into their homes. No one was hurt and the plane was later shot down.

My dad kept lots of rabbits and chickens, I used to look after them, feed water and clean them out. Dad had a big allotment where he grew all different vegetables, I used to help him and go everywhere with him, I loved him to bits and he was my best friend as well as a loving dad.

I belonged to the 22nd Eltham Guides and was Patrol Leader of the swallows. I once carried the banner in Eltham Church, I felt very important. The guides used to set the tables for breakfast for the parishioners in the Church Hall and serve their meal when they arrived.

Also while in the guides I learnt to ring the bells in Eltham Church for many Sunday worships, I was bell number 4. My mum used to get the neighbours out in the garden to listen, she was quite proud of me.

...after the war.

We as children loved to go to Eltham Swimming Pools, we used to go every Saturday morning and take a big dripping sandwich to eat when we came out.

In the winter the big pool was boarded over and made into a dance hall, and live bands played every Saturday night. The boys used to show off their Teddy Boy suits and big kipper ties, Elvis haircuts and thick soled shoes, the girls showed off their swingy dresses and jiving skills.

In the summer we would walk from Eltham Middle Park to Danson Park open air lido and spend the day there. I met my future husband there and married at 18 and had two sons Dana and Garry who still live locally, one in Welling and one in Bexley.

I have 5 grandchildren and 2 great grand children and am now living in Plumstead with my two dogs Sparky and Woody and wonderful memories of my time in Eltham.

COLD HANDS
by Miriam Storey

Cold Hands.

What was it his mother use to say about cold hands?

He watches the snow dance its way down, settling quietly on the benches outside the library. The high street is eerily quiet but for the occasional cautious crunch of a determined commuter or slushy rattle of a vehicle inching along the road. He glances up at the library, what if it doesn't open, what then? A walk, a slow snowy trudge, the Palace will look pretty, or the Tudor barn. Like living in a Christmas card his wife would have said.

Cold hands.

He stretches his fingers in his gloves.

She had loved this town, the history, the people, the shops. He smiles. He had suggested once, maybe a move, somewhere further out, a bigger house? But she had laughed gently and said ' I have everything I want right here, why go anywhere else?'

He looks up again at the library, the red brick, the stone pillars. The unassuming grandeur, familiar and ever present entity, like love, she said and she had loved this place most of all. He puts his hand on the wooden front door, it looks warm. The sudden scrape of the key in the lock takes him by surprise, as if it were his touch alone causing the mechanisms to retract.

Cold hands.

It comes to him then, what his mother use to say.

Cold hands.

As the light within spills out of the opening door, a smile.

Cold hands, warm heart.

Avery Hill Training College - Now Greenwich University

Early 1900's - High Street - Eltham

Our Animal Friends

Animals had an important place in many stories and deserved their own chapter! From pets, to imaginary elephants or pantomime horses they ran and galloped across the pages and imagination of the writers.

The winner of the children's section was the story by Beatrix Robinson 'Eltham Escape' with a delightful story with a great final twist.

Dogs played a part in many stories, but there is a most amusing story about a pet fish which must ring a chord with many parents! Some animals such as a cat may be a ghost. Even the indulged lemur Mah-Jong owned by the Courtaulds, residents of Eltham Palace in the 1930's, inspired a story.

Many familiar places are mentioned in the amusing story about a pantomime horse. Wartime and the feeding of pigs is the subject of one story.

Animals can be friends, even a wolf and ponies. They can come to the rescue of babies or show the kinder side of lads in Queenscroft.

With lions as well as birds inspiring stories, suburban Eltham is a menagerie of wildlife.

Eltham Escape
by Beatrix Robinson - age 9

The front door was open. Nobody was looking. This was my chance. I dashed out and ran up the road. When I looked back there was a man running up the road as well. Why, a full-grown man! Who did he think he was running up the road like that? Oh! I think he's that guy doing something with wires on the side of our house. I kept on running and turned onto another busier road. I ran along, the man still chasing me. I passed lots of shops with nice smells coming from them. Why, that boy's ice-cream smells good! Oh – I must not stop or the man might catch me!

I ran and ran. I ran across the road and big noisy monsters with wheels honked at me. I ran past an old wall into a yard with lots of big flat stones in it. The old stone building in the middle had a pointy bit that went "bong!" I ran past a man with smelly ankles, dodged an old lady who tried to catch me and a girl who tried to stroke me. I crossed another smaller road and saw a green building with a big yellow squiggle on it and a delicious smell coming from it.

I dodged the honkers across another road and ran down the side of a white building with black railings. Mmm what a wonderful smell... oh no, a dead end! What shall I do?

I turned around and there was the man! I tried to dodge. I really did. But he caught me. He carried me all the way home. But when I was at the bottom of the road we live on my people came running to greet me. I looked at my people, wagged my tail, cocked my ears and gave a bark. Home was the best place to be.

Little James, The Giant Mole and Cannibal Pigs

by Tony Tang

Little James sat in the garden of his next door neighbours on Glenshiel Road. Mother was working somewhere in Woolwich, "part of the war effort" Father said. Mrs. Thomas was looking after him, and was busy in the kitchen making tea while Clare, his best friend, was busy drawing dresses and colouring them in.

James was bored and wanted an adventure. He thought about the house at the end of Glenshiel Road. When he was evacuated to Granny and Aunt Barbara in New Milton, there it was standing proudly looking out at Eltham Park. When he came back a few months later it had disappeared. There was a mystery that needed to be investigated!

Curious, James walked out of the garden. He went down the road past the lampposts, where the slop buckets hung collecting waste food for the pigs. Finally he stood at the end of the road looking at a hole full of rubble, burnt timber, broken glass, and scattered clothes. He wondered what had happened to the family that lived there. There was a boy and a girl, he didn't know their names, but he played with them once. He stared at the crater. He wondered if a Giant Mole had come up and taken them away. Maybe it had eaten them. Imagine that, a giant man eating mole!

"James, Tea Time" cried Mrs. Thomas. Walking back he worried about scary man eating animals with big teeth pouncing out at him. When he got in Clare was already at the table glaring unhappily at a couple of grey looking sausages. "Yuck", she cried "give them to the pigs!" This was too much for an already stressed James. "Clare" he said sternly, "That is cannibalism and should not be encouraged!"

Funeral in Eltham

by Val Spargo

At the top of Southend Crescent, a shiny BMW lurched into a tiny Renault. 'Should have jumped the lights, dad,' said a knowing voice from the back.
'Stay there, you lot,' said the mother, struggling out of the car.
It was only after strained discussions and polite exchange of details that the water draining from the plastic fish tank became apparent.
Early next morning loud sobs reached the bedroom.
'What on earth's a matter, Alex?' said his mother.
'Goggles is dead.'
'I'm so sorry, darling. Are the others alright?' His mother opened her arms to the distressed eight year-old.
'They're fine,' said Sophie, his elder sister, carrying the large new tank containing three active and one dead goldfish.
'We'll talk about it downstairs,' said mother heading off further potential disaster.
'They're my very first pets,' wailed Alex. 'Goggles was my favourite.'
'It's probably whip-lash, after the crash,' said his sister.
'The other three look healthy, though,' reassured his mother.
'Down the loo?' said his father.
'No,' came the chorus.
The funeral was held that morning. Alex fashioned an Egyptian funeral barge from plasticine, father dug the hole, mother provided the prayer book and Sophie warbled, 'What shall we do with a drunken sailor' on her recorder. Through sniffs Alex said, 'Goodbye, Goggles. Have a good voyage to heaven'
Later a small balsa wood cross marked the spot.
On Monday morning, the floating belly of Spectacles was heralded by Alex's sobs. The funeral was less elaborate and minus father.
On Tuesday, Alex once more appeared at his parents' bedside. In one hand was a third dead goldfish, in the other, a toy spade.
'Lipstick is dead. I'm going to dig up the others and take them back to the shop. I want my money back'.

MAH-JONGY'S JOURNEY
A SHORT STORY OF A LITTLE FACT, A LOT OF FICTION AND EVEN MORE NONSENSE

by Doreen Thorogood

'Jongy, Jongy…hurry up….please jump on my back…….'
The mat was prickly and packed ……days and days went by in a haze of heat. The ocean was relentless ….storms battered our little mat until at last we were tossed ashore in a strange land – Madagascar.

That was long ago and my journey to Eltham in the far off UK was an eventful one.

In the claustrophobic, dirty cage I wondered what had happened. Snoozing one minute under a shady tree and the next the world turned upside down and I was bumping along in a box with an assortment of other creatures bound for who knew where.

Virginia and Stephen loved me. My cage, decorated with tropical scenes, reminded me of my beloved Madagascar. I even had heating in it as I come from a warm climate. The house was spectacular, set in the grounds of Eltham Palace – I had the run of it. Virginia would carry me around on her shoulder, feeding me tidbits of the finest quality.

Life was good. I felt human which was a bit confusing being a Lemur and all that.

Then everything changed. Bully came along.

A large, flatulent, lemur hating bull dog. That was the end of my charmed life at Eltham Palace. I had to leave. Heartbroken to be parted from my adorable Virginia, but to save my skin I just had to go.

With nothing to pack I slipped out during the night, took one long look back then melted away into the darkness. Under a shady tree, squinting into the sunlight back in sunny Madagascar I often wondered what happened to Virginia in far away Eltham……

Eltham Pantomime
by Paul Harton

Clip clop clip clop clip clop

It's for charity it's for a good cause it's for charity, I keep reminding myself. "Are we near Eltham High St yet?" Back end says to me from the rear. It's the first thing he has said for a couple of furlongs. Damn! I'm even thinking in horse parlance now. Mind you, being confined in this getup is hardly the inspiration for great discourse of any kind, I shouldn't think that if I had his view I would be running off at the mouth. I tell him we've just passed Alan's Furniture Shop, and heading for McDonald's, his heavy sigh tells me this hasn't consoled him.

Clip clop……clip…..clop

We begin to slow down and from my limited view from this (now rather sweaty) horse's head mask I can see we have now arrived at our destination, outside the GPO pub in Passey Place. As the volunteers walk around with their collection buckets among the busy passers by and shoppers I pause to think, what the hell am I doing here? I've never been one for charity, my whole life has been a mission of sidestepping the minefield of street fundraisers and avoiding worthy causes. Whilst Selfish was not quite my middle name, I would never be thought of as the first to step forward for a noble cause. So why was I here in my very own manor, cocooned in this costume with the manager from Sainsbury's hanging off my rear? And then I heard a familiar voice, a charming mellifluous voice and I knew why. I strain my horse's head around 90 degrees and there she is, being so utterly charming, looking so captivating, that I would have agreed to be the Back End to be near her.

Eltham Reserve
by Liz Davies

Glen Ure looked across at Eli Bank and watched the elephant school in action. The adults were teaching the calves to kick up dust with their feet. He was completely in awe of the animal world and how they all had their role in bringing up the next generation. In his 4x4 he moved on across the plain. Coming to a rocky outlet he spotted the lion he called Glen. He was a majestic beast and lazily observed all around him, keeping watch over his pride that was sheltering from the heat. Glen Ure continued on his way across the green acres. As he looked across the green vale towards Earls Hall Lodge he had never felt happier. He had worked hard to achieve his dream and had built a successful business. The Lodge was now a successful base for safari holidays and his skills as a guide were much in demand. He thought about his life and how he had fulfilled his dreams since he was that little boy growing up in the suburban district of London known as Eltham.

A Babe in Eltham Park North
by Frances O'Connor

One sunny afternoon in a semi-detached house on Dairsie Road, Ellen and Richard were setting off to take their dog Ollie for a walk to Eltham Park North to feed the ducks at the duck pond, the walk through the woods to Eltham Park South.

After feeding the ducks they played Frisbee with Ollie as the piggie in the middle. "Let's go and get an ice cream " suggested Richard "Good idea " Ellen replied. So the three of them set off through the woods to Eltham Park South, they'd get their ice cream from the cafe there.

As they got to the middle of the woods they heard a high pitched wailing sound. "What's that?" said Richard. "I don't know, but I don't like it" replied Ellen. Ollie ran off towards the sound. "May be it's a fox" said Richard. "Ollie come back " shouted Ellen, but he didn't and they ran after him.

Ollie was standing by a pram, Ellen and Richard walked over and peered into it, there laying in it was a baby staring "Someone's left their baby, what should we do" said Ellen. I've got my phone I'll Google the number of Eltham Police Station " suggested Richard. The number came up so Richard made the call.

After a long conversation with the Safer Neighbourhood Team Richard explained to Ellen that the baby had been left by its elder siblings who had got side tracked playing in the woods, then lost their way. They had gone to the cafe at Eltham Park South to report their missing sibling and were waiting there with members of the Safer Neighbourhood Team.

So Ellen, Richard and Ollie took the baby to them and it was ice creams all round.

Cats and Dogs!
by Tessa Cheek

It was a balmy and relaxing springtime in Eltham. The garden was green and shady with a gentle sound of bees buzzing amongst the flowers.

Ben and Jaz were visiting. They were well-behaved, loveable dogs. Ben was friendly and confident. His chocolate coloured coat was curly. His deep brown eyes pleaded, "please play with me." Jaz was smooth-haired and golden, quivering with nervousness. Her eyes begged for love and kindness. Both dogs enjoyed our walks in the park, and we became very fond of them.

Zach and Lucy were our resident cats. Zach was a placid, affectionate tabby, but Lucy was quicksilver, alert and lively. She had smooth, glossy brownish-blond fur and strangely golden eyes, suggesting a trace of Burmese in her parentage.

Zach ignored the doggy intruders as he snoozed contentedly in the sunshine, but Lucy was wary whenever Ben or Jaz came too close. Ben often approached playfully, but Zach took no notice and Lucy hissed as she retreated!

One peaceful Sunday morning we opened all the windows wide and we breakfasted in the garden. Our cats relaxed in the sun….too much! Ben bounded up and with a bloodcurdling yowl Lucy shot right through the house, and out of the skylight window onto the roof. We gasped as she scrambled precariously to the chimney ledge. At first no gentle reassurance could sooth her terror as in vain we stretched from the window towards her, but much later she began wailing pitifully. The roof looked too steep to descend but Lucy remained beyond our reach!

A dilemma indeed, but for our compassionate Eltham fire brigade! Rescuing Lucy was not a problem, the fireman said, as he handed a trembling ball of fur to us that afternoon in exchange for our grateful donation to the benevolent fund!

Wolfy and Jessica

by Annalise Webber - age 7

One day a little girl named Jessica was strolling through Well Hall. She saw a white baby wolf. So Jessica was not frightened. Jessica and the baby wolf played together. Meanwhile the mummy and daddy wolf were coming home. When the mummy and daddy came home they were cross. Luckily the baby wolf knew what to do. The baby wolf called out. Wolfy said to his mum and dad "that little girl is my friend". "Well" said daddy wolf "if she is your friend we will not hurt her". Jessica could understand and talk animal language. So she said "thank you, shall we play some more?" "Yes" said Wolfy. Then they all went to play together. Wolf mummy and daddy, Wolfy and Jessica. Jessica and Wolfy visit each other every day now. And they live happily ever after.

QUEENSCROFT
by Antonia Robinson

The mother struggles to cross the road. She holds the toddler's hand, pushing the buggy, dog-lead looped over one handle. The baby howls with hunger and the afternoon's scrubbed blue skies are staining with cloud. "Dear God please get us to the playground so the older one can run about while I nurse baby" she pleads between gritted teeth. Puppy pulls on the lead: the pram wobbles precariously. She can't get to the park quickly enough.

Passing the empty paddling pool she wonders if they'll ever get it working again. "It would be lovely for the children in the summer..." Distracted, she notes a group of young men on the swings. Eyes dart around to see if there are any other families in the park. There aren't. Hopes the teens are the friendly sort.

A playground stand-off: Mother and teenage boys, eyes locked. Cigarettes behind ears, the cultivated nonchalance of youth meets its match in sleep-deprived maternal instinct.

For a very long moment even the trees hold their breath.

Then in one fluid motion the lanky one in converse and baseball cap leaps towards the pushchair shouting "Here you lot, clear this up – or he'll get hurt!"

The others follow their leader and scrabble around picking up the bits of broken glass on the ground. The mother hadn't noticed it. The last shard collected, lanky lad turns to her astonished face, beaming. "That's better, it's all safe now. He could have got cut on the glass, that's dangerous that is."

She follows his gaze not to her son toddling towards the slide, nor to the baby in the pushchair, but to the small, white Roman-nosed creature sitting at the end of the lead gazing rapt at his new admirers. "I love Bull Terriers I do, and that's one wicked puppy you've got there Miss".

Am I Imagining?
by Georgie Hawkins - age 11

BEEP! BEEP! BEEP! My alarm clock burned my ears hard. I buried my head into my pillow and quickly hit the snooze button. No noise, finally. I jumped out of my bed and into my fluffy, pink slippers. I opened my bedroom door and looked around at the flat. Silence… Mum and dad were still in bed. I sat down on the tattered sofa and ate a crunchy, green apple. I thought about going on an adventure, not that I could go on an adventure in my life…

I crossed the road near Gregg's. I could smell the sweet taste of the iced donuts in the window. My tummy started to rumble as I smelt the delicious food in the shop. I just ignored it and carried on walking down the road, as I did not have any money. As I walked past pound land I came to an ally. A damp ally… a cold ally… a… mysterious ally. I stopped and looked down it. I could hear a voice. It was like a laugh of some kind, like one I had never heard. I walked towards the end of it. It kept getting bigger, like it was moving. Then I looked to my right and saw a large, tall, wooden door. It had a black, metal handle. A chill ran down my spine like a snake. I took a deep breath and opened the door as scared as an animal in a cage.

It was a whole new world, with luminous flowers and vibrant trees. Three little animals came up to me: a white spotted blue bird, a cute orange rabbit and the most tiniest mouse I had ever seen, as red as roses. I said to myself "am I imagining?…"

The Rustle in the Trees in Eltham

by Katie Geogiou - age 11

The wind hit Eltham like an atomic bomb had hit it. Katherine quickly poked her head out the window looking quite star struck. She carried on watching her film. She thought she had been imagining it, until she heard another rattle in the tree again. Funny enough she was to suspicious to carry on.

She shouted down to her mother and told her the problem. Her confused mother thought she was joking, like usual, but this time Katherine was telling the truth. Now this was getting weird first the rustle in the tree of Eltham and now Katherine telling the truth! Wow, what a day. At this time mum was extremely worried too. Mum instructed Katherine not to wake up Ella, Joanne, Andre and Zola up until she gets their father.

Dad wasn't too happy to hear the unfortunate news. Whilst father and mother were discussing the situation Katherine went to get her brothers and sisters up. The children snuck out the white front door and through the wooden porch door once their parent had realised, their dad raced after them with is huge shiny ladder on his shoulder whilst mother followed after them. Dad gave in and finally helped he opened the silver ladder and started to climb it. As he reached the middle of the tree he heard a little quiet tweet. They discovered it was a homeless injured baby blue bird. They decided to keep and care for the small unfortunate blue bird Joanne and Katherine cared for it; Ella and Andre feed it mother, father and Zola washed it and everyone named it RUSTLE!

The Friendship Ponies
by Kaelyn Okai - age 8

Once upon a time there was a town called Eltham. All the people were angry with each other. In a different world there was a town called Ponyvill, it had lots of ponies like Twilight, Rainbowdash, Applejack, Pinkie Pie, Vairity, Fluttershine and a baby dragon called Spike. There was also a princess called princess Selestia. She was very upset that all the people were fighting so she sent them to the other world. When they got there they were very different looking. They ended at Eltham High Street when they got to the end of Eltham everybody was fighting like crazy.

So they sang a song to make them understand about friendship. When they finished the song they were all calm and happy.

Found in Eltham

by Sofia Drake Parella - age 9

Long ago the fingertips of dawn shone through the trees. Lenny the lion yawned. His mouth was so big, like a small cave lined with ferocious, huge, shiny teeth. When Lenny woke up, he had such a shock. He was in what seemed to be the worst place in the world, the human land!. He was terrified but also puzzled. How did he end up there when he was sleeping peacefully in his cave with Ma lion, Pa lion and Sister lion?

He got up and carefully walked through the empty streets. Hours passed and soon, people started filling the streets but the lonely, lost lion stayed hidden in the shadows.

As Lenny listened to people, he heard them mentioned a place called the Tudor Barn. So that is where he was. He started to get extremely hungry but had no idea how to get food so he decided to ask a friendly looking pigeon sitting on a low branch.

"Excuse me", interrupted Lenny, "do you know how I can get some food?". The pigeon, called Peter, was startled when he saw a lion in the Tudor Barn. "What are you doing here?", he asked. Lenny told him that he had no idea how he had arrived to this 'Barn'. They had a long conversation and Lenny learned how to get some food.

As he walked towards a group of people eating, they saw him and screamed. The noise echoed through Lenny's ears. Someone had called the zookeeper because before he knew it, a huge net flung over his head.

Lenny closed his eyes and heard a voice: "Lenny, wake up". He opened his eyes and was back in his cave with Sister lion. It had all been a nightmare and what a nightmare!. So relieved it was all over!.

The Mystery Cat
by Natasha Wren - age 11

I looked at it. It looked at me. Something strange was drawing me closer to it. I could only see its warm, golden eyes but I already knew it would not hurt me. When it came into the light, out from the bushes in the Eltham Palace gardens, I could see it was a cat. A plain, black cat. I knew a lot about cats but I've never had one. My mum would always say "Patricia, I told you time and time again that we just can't look after a cat." And that would be the end of that. She used to own a black cat called Timmy when she was a child. She loved that cat more than anything. One day, she came home from school to hear that he had died of old age. She promised herself that she would never get another cat because no one could replace Timmy.

Suddenly I noticed how skinny the cat was and he didn't have a collar either, so he couldn't have had an owner? I patted him on the head and walked away, into the main art-deco house to catch up with mum. He didn't follow me.

Yet it was on the following day, walking back from Crown Woods College that I saw him again. Maybe mum would let me keep him? I knew it was him because of his golden eyes and that's when I realised. It looked so much like Timmy - Mum had shown me pictures. I knew it was silly because Timmy died years ago but I decided to see if he would respond. I called him. He came over to me but when I reached out to stroke him, my hand went right through him. It was definitely Timmy. But Timmy was a ghost.

81

1930 - Greetings From Eltham Postcard

War Memorial - Eltham

A Victorian Murder
1871

In 1871 there was a murder in Eltham of a servant girl which hit the headlines of the day and inspired writers to this day.

The horror of the murder is brought home by many stories. The language used in stories is graphic and invokes a bygone era of Victorian times. Some stories are from the viewpoint of the policemen of the time as he walked the streets with his lantern and the gruesome find.

The story still haunts the area. One story brings it up to date with the air of mystery in her story. The horror of the discovery by the Victorian policemen is described in the stories in the stories by the children writers.

Was Edmund the killer? Was there an issue of class and power? Does her ghost still roam in Kidbrooke Lane? You decide.

There was no justice for Jane, but she is remembered in the writing of these short stories which maybe can act as a memorial to her.

April is the Cruellest Month
by Reeva Charles

She kicked the gravel as she trudged unhappily down the path in the rose garden. Spring was perking up all around in the Well Hall Pleasaunce with April marching in its best blossom. 'David can go hang himself,' she thought, 'I don't care.' But she did. She was more worried though about having just lost her waitressing job - her misery compounded by the joyful sunny scene all around her. Following the moat around the old Tudor Barn, she found herself on the grass gazing out through the railings and onto Kidbrooke Lane.

It was then she heard it. A faint cry at first and then, "My poor head, just let me die". She looked around suspiciously. What was that? But she could see no one. Breathless now, she looked around desperately. She saw a young man walking away from her.

"Oi," she shouted, "Did you hear that?"

He turned and looked curiously at her. As he slowly took a step towards her, she could see he was wearing some sort of uniform – yes, a printing firm, with the name badge proudly declaring, "Ted Pook." Strange name, she thought.

"Nah, didn't hear nuffin".

He shuffled off looking a bit embarrassed, avoiding her gaze.

"Oh god," she thought, he thinks I'm stalking him or am some kind nutter.

She put her strange experience down to the wind, or maybe her dark mood. She'd better get home and check the jobs websites.

She turned sharply, the wind catching her face, electrifying her hair when a stray piece of paper flew up against her body refusing to retreat. She peeled it off. It was a torn newspaper page. She read its words with growing horror: "The Eltham Murder - A young servant girl was found murdered in Kidbrooke Lane…" It was dated April 1871.

The Eltham Case
by Joanne Walby

Darkness, broken only by vague gaslight from the street beyond and me lantern I always carry on duty at such an hour. Ten after two in the morning and I was on my way back from patrol when the peaceable silence shattered with that scream. She lay strewn across muddy Kidbrooke lane, Sunday best shredded, bonnet I knew not where; blood pooled in the light as she clutched her head. As she raised herself and crawled towards me, I could not but gasp at the horror. She died four days later.

He was never brought to justice, even at the Old Bailey. Them as never are, son of a Printer for the Times. It was a love affair of course, though he swore infatuation on her part. Doctor who received her at St Thomas's said she had been with child, so can't have been that one-sided. Spoilt good for nothing second son, singing in the local taverns, always at the music-hall; prone to fits so as to explain the mud he brushed off his trousers in the nearby sweet shop on his way home. Nothing to explain the blood hastily washed from his shirt cuffs.

Had his way with her and panicked at the thought of a child. That's what I say. Wouldn't disappoint his prospects or his mother with an untoward marriage. Couple passed by and heard screaming but thought it merely "horse-play". And her, a maid in his Father's house sacked two weeks before, for what reason? None as I can find makes sense.

There was a pamphlet condemning his guilt, even a float upon which actors recreated the crime. But all for nothing. He went into hiding, made a moderate marriage some ten years later, once the furore had subsided. Good luck to her I say.

Wading Through the Dewy Grass
by Isabella Fuller - age 10

Wading through the dewy grass, the damp air was a wrath; around my shoulders, I checked my pocket watch; half three am. The atmosphere was spine tingling as April wind danced through the trees, and slowly I began to feel sleepy. My woollen police coat wasn't providing enough heat, but yet again I had only an hour left. Either way it didn't look like it would be light soon.

Silence bordered me.

I was coming close to the end of my shift I felt a change of surface underneath my rubber boot. My light towered above a glove. Then a hat followed by a rasping rattling voice….

Moving my lamplight, I caught a sight of leather boots. On the soft damp grass was a sorrowful young girl moaning.

Footsteps surrounded me.

"Oh my poor head, my poor head "she mumbled under a gust of wind, I noticed a gash on her head deep enough to see her brain protruding from her head.

Was the case ever solved?

On that night she was taken to Guys Hospital to seek further medical attention. Sadly she never regained consciousness and died on Sunday April 30th. Her alarmed uncle identified her as his niece; Jane Maria Clousen, on the 1st May. She was a maid working for the Pook family In Greenwich. A few days before she died a hammer was found in the grounds of Morden Collage, this was thought to be the murder weapon; on the 27th April. Mr Pook was taken to Coroners court and then escorted to Old Bailey where he was tried not guilty …

So if at night you hear blood curdling screams and you spot a young lady In Victorian clothes, there Is a chance you have seen Jane; she will not rest until justice Is served.

THE GHOST OF KIDBROOKE LANE

by Koren Ozmus - age 11

25th April 1871
3:30am
Eyes tired after a long shift, I stood in the lonely, dark, muddy forest breathing the cold foggy air. I could hear nothing but my quickening heartbeat. Pulling out my pocket watch, I was relieved to see that I only had an hour left of my shift but as I turned to go back to the station my lamplight stumbled upon a pair of light tanned gloves lying close to a damp woollen hat. Moaning alerted me to the present of another person. The hairs on the back of my neck were standing to attention as a shiver ran down my spine. Suddenly my light caught glimpse of a leg…

Despite the mud that was like quick sand, I stood there staring at a young looking girl; she was dressed in a high neck blouse attached to a long wooden skirt above a pair of button up boots. She faintly muttered to me "oh my poor head" I had noticed she had wet blood dripping down her cheek and a cut on the other. Would the murderer ever give in?

Sunday 30th April
Jane Maria Clousen, a 17 year old girl who was a maid for the Pook family sadly past away at Guys hospital, on 27th April, the murder weapon (a hammer) was found in the gardens of Morden College encrusted with rusty, dark, blood. On 1st May, Jane was identified by her Uncle William Trott. Edman Walter Pook was arrested for the murder of Jane and was taken to coroner's court where he was found guilty then to the Old Baileys where he was found not guilty. If you ever happen to walk past Kidbrooke Lane I suggest you run! She will not rest until justice is served.

25TH APRIL 1871

by Maisie Hook - age 11

Stomping my way through the damp mud, the wind was blowing against my face. I was trying to guide my way through the darkness with my dim police light. I checked the time; 3:45am not long until my shift was over. Suddenly, I stumbled across a long cream glove, I didn't think anything of it. I looked around and there on the ground was a brown hat; I realised I wasn't alone.

Starting to move my flashlight across the grass when I caught a glimpse of a mysterious object; a high collared blouse. My mind must be playing tricks on me. There in-front of me was a young girl on her hands and knees. I could hear her moaning faintly "My poor head. Oh my poor head". Blood was pouring out of her head on to her dark skirt. Her last words that she ever said were "let me die". I needed help from an Ostler so I ran.

Was the case ever solved?

I took the girl to Guys hospital where she never regained consciousness. On 30th April she died. The next day she was identified by her uncle William Trott, who worked down the docks as a lighter man. He revealed that the girl was 17 and called Jane Maria Coulson. A hammer covered in blood-stains was found outside Morden College and man named Edmund Walter Pook was arrested. Jane had worked for Edmunds family as a maid, she had said that she was marrying Edmund. It was trialed at the Old Bailey and Edmund was found not guilty.

Nobody has ever been found guilty. So if you are walking down Kidbrooke Lane then listen out for horrific screams. "may Gods great pity touch his heart and leave my murderer to confess his dreadful deed".

The Spirit of Jane
by Sinem Ozturk - age 11

Eyes tired, the only sound creaking branches, as I started to begin my long night shift. I could feel the damp, wet mud touching to tips of my toes. Breathing in the damp, wet grass with taste of decaying wood tingling my tonsils. The comfort of my coat keeping me warm as the rain sped down like a herd of bulls, time, time was my main enemy.4:09am. I wondered if anything would happen throughout my boredom. Rustling in the bushes come suddenly; in that instant I knew I wasn't alone.

Slowly, relighting my lamp,the light had blinded my eyes. I heard a shriek and the Lamp dropped. Long cream gloves sat beside the road, and 2ft away, I saw a woollen hat. My light caught a glimpse of a sudden glow beside the road; a young women with a white high-neck blouse. Looking back at what I found, I realised that a young women, sixteen or maybe eighteen, was lying against a bush (with a buttoned up boots). A shiver ran down my spine as I saw a clear vision of a young woman. Right cheek bleeding with bright red blood, It seemed surreal, this must had been a deep cut.

Would anyone ever feel guilty? Days later after the horrifying find, the young women who had been taken to Guy's Hospital had terribly lost her life. Her distraught uncle, a lighterman, identified her as Jane Maria Clousen, seventeen year old women. William Trot was his name. Monday evening someone had been arrested, for the death. Jane worked for Edward Pook's father as a maid, he was taken to the Old Bailey and was found as not guilty.

May God's great pity touch his heart and lead my murder to confess his dreadful deed. Beware. Beware.

It Was a Dark and Windy Night
by William Quilter - age 11

It was a dark and windy night; trees rustling. Walking through the deserted forest, I pulled out my pocket watch to see how long I had left of my shift; 3:40am. Begging for the time to tic by. I realised I had an hour to go still. I began to walk to walk on to see if anything was happening; When I came across something very unusual; a strange glove lying on the ground. It looked like it belonged to someone. Nervously I went to pick it up. As I did so all I heard was a massive scream!

Standing still I looked around to see if anyone was about. At first I saw nothing, but a closer look revealed a girl lying on the ground. Shocked, I tried to help her but all she mumbled was "my poor head". I was silent as I began to notice blood puddles surrounding the girl like an island. I pleaded to her let me help you but all she muttered was "let me die". I ran to Well Hall farm to try and find a Osler to help the girl.

Would anyone ever fell guilty? Sadly, despite being sent to Guy's Hospital she never regained consciousness. She died on Sunday the 30th of April. Her uncle, William Trotter, identified her as Jane Maria Clousen, a maid who worked for the Pook family. Edmund Walter Pook was arrested for murder, after a blood stained hammer was found. The shopkeeper Identified Edmund, who was sent to the coroners court for trial at the old bailey where, surprisingly, he was found not guilty. Nobody has ever been found guilty of Janes murder. On her tombstone it will say may gods great pity touch his heart and lead my murderer to confess his dreadful deed.

An Eltham Street in the Snow

The Tudor Barn - Eltham

GHOSTS AND FANTASTICAL GOINGS ON

Imagination was encouraged when writing about An Eltham Experience. This produced a fantastic selection of ghost stories all set in Eltham, many in familiar places. Eltham Church, schools, Eltham Palace, homes and local shops are all settings for the Eltham ghost stories. Even the white Greenwich University bus which takes students between campuses and a funfair are places where there are ghostly happenings. Stories are scary and often funny.

Sometimes strange things happen in Eltham... well they do in our stories. Computers are taken over, tidal waves envelop the area, children are bounced into space, abducted by aliens, there are murders mysteries on trains, time machines take children back to Tudor times and we have fairies in Eltham Palace.

So when you walk around Eltham... beware. You don't know what will happen.

The Ghost of Eltham Church
by Liam Fitzpatrick

The brilliant glow, of a full moon, bathed the churchyard silently and gently, as if by some design and intention. A scene both seen and unseen, by so many in all the many centuries, since the church of John The Baptist, had marked the high point of Eltham.

He hoped he wouldn't be noticed, as he stealthily, opened the creaking wooden gate, that led to a footpath, and then the many gravestones, with their weathered, illegible inscriptions. The oldest, reading more like coded hieroglyphic, only having meaning to those who lived back then.

He could hear when deep within the churchyard, more muted now, the sounds of cars and people, going to and fro, on the high street behind him, becoming more otherworldly, unaware and not knowing, of this secret quiet place. Yet there it was, at the centre of the vibrant, noisy heart.

The silhouette of a squirrel, sat motionless and poised, atop a grey and moss-marked stone tablet. He could just make out, the years of 1789 and 1833 inscribed.

"When e'er the bell chimes, think on me, and passing time "

With eyes half-closed, in the inadequate moonlight, and moving nearer to the stone, he heard the loud cavernous chime, of the church bell resonate and fill the still chilly air, with sound. Just one, no more, and almost frozen to where he stood, he looked anxiously to the tower, half-hoping, frantic, to see a reassuring light within.

There was no light, in the bell tower, nor anywhere within, and no movement. Just a darkness, that pervaded every stone and space. He quickly turned and ran. Back in the light and sounds of the high street. He told no one of this night, but remembers when he passes, the passing of time, and those long gone.

CTRL-ELT-DEL

by Anna Cookson

It wasn't until I got my new PC home from Eltham High Street that I noticed the strange button, next to 'Alt.'

'Elt.'

Curiosity pulsed. I tried it, but nothing happened. So I tried this: 'Control Elt Delete.'

The day caved in and the walls caved out, and, suddenly, I was in the middle of a wood, trees reaching upwards, all around.

A man, dragging a large clock behind him, was muttering to himself. I asked him; 'where am I?"

"Why, Elt-spam of course!" Indignantly, he lugged the timepiece off again.

I walked and I walked until I recognised Kidbrooke's flats, tall in the evening sun. I walked and I walked until I saw Sidcup, coursing with commuters... but in-between, only trees with gnarled knowing branches.

Eltham was gone, and, I noticed, my watch had gone too; a mark where the strap had been.

Looking around for help, there was only a brown muddy path and a sign saying: "Well Small," with an arrow pointing nowhere.

I hadn't a Bob Hope of getting back to normality.

That's when the computer gleamed electronic guilt in the orange sunset; quiet, canny, and culpable.

So I tried pushing all the buttons in all the orders, but the trees gathered around me, rubbing their leaves, telling me I was wrong.

After a while, the man dragging the huge clock came back. He peered at the screen, sweating with the effort of dragging his big watch and said; "have you tried turning it on and off again?"

The day caved out and the walls caved in, and, suddenly, I was back home.

That's when my Mum looked up from 'Whoogle' and said, "did you know the inventor of the wrist watch came from Eltham? John Arnold, he used to live in Well Hall."

The White Bus
by John Wingham

He had gone to the Thursday night jazz club as usual and had a couple of pints but he hadn't felt well all evening. He'd left early and had started to walk home down the high street. It wasn't far and he had done it many times. His left arm had felt funny and he had a pain in his chest that wouldn't go away.

He had gone in the Park Tavern for a small whiskey thinking it would help but the pains had got worse. Some of the regulars had offered to take him home but he valued his independence and had refused. How he wished he had taken up their offer. He was in agony now, and found breathing difficult. He looked around for help but the high street was deserted.

Then he saw it, the white bus. It was the one the students used to get from their campus in Eltham to Greenwich. It was slowing down. How odd, he thought, it never stops just goes back and forth up the high street.

The bus drifted silently forward its lights dim. It seemed not quite solid. He rubbed his eyes as it came to a stop beside him, its doors hissed invitingly open. He hesitated, it seemed strange, not quite right. As he stepped on board all the pain melted away. Surprised he dropped his coat on the pavement. But it didn't matter anymore. As he took his seat he knew that this was the last bus ride he would ever take.

The Montbelle Ghost

by Alan Moc - age 10

"Class dismissed!" snapped Mrs Jaw. Fred was a wimp; he was the wimpiest kid in the entire school. He was teased for being scared of the dark (scared of everything). Fred had a few friends, well two were imaginary. He had a reputation for being frightened.

"Hey Fred!" blurted Joe, running after him.

Joe was Fred's trustworthy friend, he helped him try overcoming his fear and unfortunately nothing worked. "Have you heard about the teacher's ominous ghost? It had been roaming the school for years," questioned Joe, hiding a smirk. "Ha so funny!" replied the wimp sarcastically.

The next day, Fred completed his ordinary morning routine and headed off to school early, for literacy boosters. Eventually, after ten minutes of walking he arrived. He cautiously walked in, heart pounding heavily. The school was a empty giant, stretching to the sky. He entered, eyes alert for sudden movements. Fred was early; he sat silently at his desk growing impatient. Something strange was happening. Groaning noises came closer. A shadowy figure approached the doors and locked it, leaving him stuck inside.

All he could do was panic. Fred knew this school as well as he knew his mother. He climbed the vent, quick as a flash. Exhausted he climbed into the D.T room where he set up camp (well that's what he called it). He had every resource needed in here weapons and protection. The wimp barricaded the door with everything he could find. Soft sobbing came from under the tables, he ran for dear life, destroying the barricade. He managed to escape the wrath of the dark figure.

After some time of cheater-pace running he arrived at his house, fortunately losing the ghost. He collapsed in his bed, tired. He grew weary. A dark figure appeared in the mirror.

The Funfair
by Amina Khan - age 11

It's all gone there is nothing left. I should have never gone to that stupid funfair. A tear fell from my eye, as I heard police sirens outside my house.

I was walking home from school one day when I saw a flickering, bright light in the corner of my eye. It was a funfair. I rushed home to go and tell mum. She said I could go on Saturday, at 6:00, with my BFF lily.

Finally, Saturday came. I brushed my teeth and ran down the stairs anxious to eat my breakfast. I had honey cheerios, with chocolate pancakes and a strawberry milkshake. After I got dressed, mum took me to Lily's house.

The clock rang. It was six o'clock.

As we entered, I could see all the rides. It was amazing; there was even a clown. "Welcome to the funfair, you may find some surprises…," he said, looking like he hated his job. We walked past the cotton candy stall but lily said we should go on the big wheel first. When she spotted the popcorn stall, she immediately changed her mind. "Oh look! I'll get some popcorn while you wait here, see you in a sec", she said happily.

When I turned around to see Lily, suddenly I felt a dark shadow creeping over my shoulder. I turned round to see the clown. He looked at me with a freaky smile. He grabbed my arm and took me into red and white striped tent. There was nothing there except Lily dead on the floor bleeding…

The Ghost of Eltham

by Arran O'Leary - age 10

Charlie was outraged. Bill had just come back with devastating news; that old delirious money loving brat, Woods had refused to lend him any money. Now, he and his other four brothers were sitting there solemnly.

Patrick's heath was getting worse every second and they all knew he wouldn't survive much longer. The following day Patrick died. The four remaining brothers weren't going to forgive Edward Woods. The next the day they made sure that Edward would beg for mercy.

Silence.... Edward Woods was starting to have an ominous feeling that something was wrong. There was something else in the room, he was sure of it. As he tentatively strode up the stairs everything seemed paranormal. When he went into his room he thought he heard a soft moaning sound. He thought nothing of it. When he lay down on his luxurious bed he was sure he heard voices. He again thought nothing of it.

Then he saw something hidden by the cloak of darkness. This time he knew he wasn't imaging things. This time he cried, just a little soft whimper, but nonetheless, a cry. After that he heard a loud bang. Woods hid under his bed sheets in fear. It was amazing how such an important, serious and respected man could be so easily reduced to nothing.

Charlie was enjoying this. He never felt more alive, he had become drunk on the sweet taste of revenge. As Michael terrorised the squirming wreck of Woods, the mocking words of Jack gave him power. Bills laughter put the cherry on the cake. Woods had enough; he slithered out under the bed and jumped out of the open window landing with a splat on the cold, hard ground.

They say Woods wanders the streets of Eltham seeking his foes.

Billy and Alice's Adventure

by Brooke Francis - age 11

One damp cold winter's night two beautiful twins were born. One of the twins was a little boy, he was named Billy and he grew up to be a very inquisitive little boy. But on the other hand, his sister was adventures and loved taking risks. On a gloomy night Billy and Alice went to their grandmother's house for a sleepover, their grandmother lived in Eltham, in a warm flat. Once Billy and Alice's parents had dropped them off, they noticed a funny, a mysterious noise coming from the attic. Both Billy and Alice took one large step towards the attic and turned the handle slowly. They took the tinniest step into the massive attic, they heard dripping noises coming from the dark and dusty windows. They ran towards the window and peered out of it. Then they saw a mysterious shadow in the middle of massive room then ran towards it and ran straight to the shadow. And steered around the gigantic attic, then ran straight downstairs to their grandmother and shouted" HELP HELP ". Their grandmother was in a deep sleep so they ran back up to the attic and stopped, at the old rusty door the door opened slowly and the shadow appeared in the middle of the attic and said "my name is Toby ". Billy and Alice didn't know if they should trust Toby but then with one blink of the eye Alice was gone. Billy looked everywhere under the table at Sainsbury's everywhere but then Billy heard a scream come from the alley way and ran straight towards it. And sitting in the corner was Alice and the ghost was gone for ever and no one ever saw him again.

Molly's Dream Comes True
by Caitlin Barcoe - age 10

"Go away Molly". I walked away down the long dark corridor. As I stepped outside into Eltham Palace Gardens I saw a hole hidden behind the rose bush. I rushed over to see what it was, but as I stared at it someone or something pushed me down it. I screamed at the top of my lungs, but I was alone. When I came to the bottom of the hole, there were lots of little faces of plants and creatures staring at me. I didn't know what to say so I just stood there staring, looking baffled. We all stood there for 5 minutes until a caterpillar slid up my leg and said "come with me to Eltham underworld".

I trotted along the blue sparkly path until we came upon a sign saying 'Forest of the West and Forest of the East'. I looked down at the strange creatures and they all pointed at the forest of the west. I nodded in appreciation and headed to the west. I turned back and waved goodbye to the creatures and carried on walking. Two hours went by until I came to a giant castle which was covered in all black. I tiptoed into the castle, but then suddenly the door slammed and I was trapped. I looked around and saw a witch holding Jodie. I stared at her and demanded that the witch would have to give her back. The witch cackled with laughter and said "I'll give you your sister back if you give me your bow." I held the bow in front of me, grabbed Jodie and took the bow with me. We ran back to Eltham Palace and me and Jodie will never ever forget this adventure.

The Haunted Room
by Chelsea Williams - age 11

RINGGGG!!! The bell went at the end of the first day back at school.

There is a legend that there are 2 nasty little girls living somewhere in the DT room in Montbelle School. That is why the light is always on.

One day 2 new girls called Lucy and Lexie, who had brown hair, brown eyes and to let know they are twins, came to Montbelle School. They had lots of fun and met lots of new friends. Lexie, Lucy and their new friends were on their way to the bathroom when Lexie said, 'Look, that light is on. Mum always says to turn out the lights.'

'Yes it wastes electric in the house,' Lucy said with amazement.

Lexie was about to turn out the light when suddenly, 'NOOO!' her friends shouted, 'they'll get you!'

'Who will get us?' Lucy and Lexie asked.

'The 2 ugly, rotten nasty twins will get you; they will take you and kill you and you'll never be seen again,' the girls exclaimed.

But Lucy and Lexie did not listen so they kept walking on.

The girls went into the DT room and turned the lights off.

SLAM!!! Suddenly the door closed behind them.

'Ok girls, good joke. You got us, now open the door,' the girls begged.

'It is not us, look behind you!' their friends warned.

'What? What's behind us? Is it the evil twins coming to get us?' they said sarcastically. The friends heard a scream. It was Lucy and Lexie.

It is 2 years later and the girls have not told anyone since Lucy and Lexie were killed in the DT room.

WHO KNOWS THEY MIGHT BE COMING FOR YOU NEXT!!

Mrs Almond?
by Demmie Jacobs - age 11

Dear Diary,
It all started when I did not believe Lucy, and the odd tales she told about Mrs Almond. It was a casual day at Haimo, or so I thought it was.

One of my friends called Bella had a mysterious death, I found her on the second floor steps dead! Her eyes were wide open, she was looking almost straight at me then suddenly I felt shivers up my spine and felt a soft whisper in my ear saying,

"Bye, I'll miss you…" Strangely no one was there, just me. I felt a warm hand on my shoulder.
"She fell down the stairs and never woke up." whispered Mrs Almond.

I used to be bullied, until Bella, the nicest, funniest, prettiest person I have ever met came and she always stuck up for me, but ever since she has died I have started to get bullied again. Every night I cry myself to sleep, the only thing that keeps me going is that for some unknown reason, I always felt Bella was with me. Every time I walk up and down the stairs I feel shivers, I feel breathless on my way downstairs to check the security cameras to look at how Bella died, I often look, the strange thing is when she fell it looked more like she had been pushed because she was four footsteps at least from the top of the stairs. I couldn't see anyone push her either, so what really happened on the day of Bella's death? I decided that someone or something killed Bella that day and I was determined to prove what really happened.

14 weeks and 17 days I have been trying to find out what happened, but still nothing. Continuously, strange things have been happening to me, I have been getting stuck in Debenhams' left, I have heard threatening voices in my head saying, "Keep away from the fields of Eltham!" After a few more weeks, I knew this mystery was impossible to solve.

One day walking down the stairs I immediately stopped, there was a boy in front of me walking first, then I saw a little girl sitting in the corner curled up in a ball, she stared at the boy then she went, "uuuuugghhhhuuuu" screamed, then the boy was gone! She was sitting there rocking, I heard her saying my name.

"Lola, Lola, Lola, Lola, Lola…" She whispers softly, I get closer and closer to the girl, then… "Bella It's you! Oh My God you're a-a-a a ghost!" I yelled.
"Don't worry, I won't hurt you …If you stop" she replied.
"Stop what?" I asked confused.
"Investigating, I got pushed by Mrs Almond, don't ask me why, then I was possessed by a demon ghost and begun to kill innocents, but if you carry on I will kill you too!" I ran and ran but she caught me and then I was gone! When I finally believed the tales Lucy had been telling me…

I woke up. I was dreaming!

The Ghost of McDonalds
by Francis Tweneboa - Koduah - age 8

One morning in Sainsburys, Mario was having a good day and was happy because he had a lot of money. Mario heard something but nobody was there. It was not his friend so who was it? Somebody was saying "Here are some cards Mario" but Mario still didn't answer. He thought there might be a queue but there was nothing. It was just his friend behind him trying to give him some football cards.

Then after work he went to McDonalds to have some tasty chips, chicken nuggets and an amazing strawberry milk shake. A little while later some of his friends came to McDonalds to have a drink, talk to Mario and play 4 or 5 games of cards but they forgot that McDonalds was going to close in about five minutes. So when they were going to leave they saw that the door closed. They were knocking on the shiny window but nobody saw them, so Mario and his friends were stuck in McDonalds.

When they were knocking on the door they heard a sound. They turned and saw a white thing shaped like a Ghost. They also heard the same sound as before from the round white thing. They thought it was a Ghost but they knew that Ghosts weren't real. But they were wrong- it was a Ghost! Mario and his friends were starting to get scared, so scared that they were running everywhere but when they looked the other way the Ghost was still following them. So the Ghost said "hey let's play a game" then Mario and his friends stopped and asked "do you really want to play?" The Ghost said "yes", so they all played with each other happily, forever and together.

Ghosts

by Gabriele Zebrauskaite - age 10

Rose opened the wooden creaky gate, gingerly she looked around to see old, flaky graves surrounding her. She stepped forward in the darkness, turning back and forth to see if anybody was following her, she couldn't believe she was going to live there.......

April 19th, it was a scary night, that day, Rose woke up feeling invisible fingers touching her back, she ran downstairs, "Hello, hello, is anybody here?" she yelled. Rose knew something was up so she went outside to check it out. Creeeeeeeak!!!!!!! The gate opened, although the birds were tweeting, it seemed like there was not a living soul there.

Rose opened the door to see herself face to face with a transparent ghost! "Help me, somebody help me!" Rose shrieked. She ran upstairs only to be faced by another ghost! Why is this happening to me, she thought to herself. She found a rusty metal door but it was locked.

Rose found a loose brick and smashed the window (leaving lots of cuts and bruises). She staggered to the gate trying to keep her balance.

Rose would never ever go back to that house again or would she.......

3 years later she passed that very same house, there was a woman quite young, but wrinkly beckoning her to come inside. She opened the very same creaky wooden gate and stepped inside the house........SLAM!

She didn't know she was a GHOST!

Ghost Night of Eltham
by Jonathan Abbott - age 11

There was a man living in Eltham on Crouch Croft road, the man was tall. He had blonde hair and he was not happy. He didn't like celebrating Christmas at all. On Christmas day he asked a boy named Jack to go and buy him a humongous chicken; and he said if he gets back in five minutes he would give him ten shillings. But when he was having a quiet sleep, suddenly he heard a noise and jumped out of bed like a frog leaping as far as it can.

Mr Abbott heard the door creak, as the ghost opened the door. He then got up and the voice said, "I'm the ghost of the past, I have come to show you about your life back in time to 1939 when you were 29. Mr Abbott went with him. "Close your eyes," said the ghost of the past. When he opened his eyes he saw himself when he was younger. He couldn't believe his eyes; he was so skinny compered to now. Mr Abbott said "get me out of here I don't want to see me anymore!" The ghost said "okay but you won't regret it there will be three ghosts haunting you!"

The ghost went and he ate the big chicken that he bought. Then he went to bed at night and it did strike at 12 o'clock and he woke up and the ghost was there and he went with him and he saw him downstairs eating a chicken and was bored. "I don't want to be here." okay then." He went and there was a ghost of future and he's the funniest and was an old man he doesn't want to be with any of them. He lived happier on his own.

THE HAUNTED MUSEUM
by Kayley Hayward - age 10

Some say it's haunted, some says it's not. The new Eltham Museum is a thrill of a life time.

Stephanie, the 15 year old girl was running down wet Eltham High Street. She looked up at the dark grey sky, when she saw her dad in the window of Eltham Palace.

Her dad had got a new job in the Eltham Palace museum. 'Dad,' she shouted. 'Dad, let me in its raining,' she shouted. He still couldn't hear her.

She went to the side of the long, quiet road and picked up a ferly big rock. She went back to the window jumped and threw it. He turned around startled. He disappeared and after a few minutes he was opening the grand doors right next to her. She walked into the magnificent museum ever.

'Why did you come here when it is pouring down with rain,' her dad said.
'I came to help you with putting the new ornaments into the museum dad,'
'We only have a few more to put down into the other room, but you can help us anyway.'

They walked up the crooked stairs when Stephanie saw the library, she wounded if she was allowed to go in there latter 'Dad, can I go into the library instead' she begged, 'Of course you can darling,' 'Thanks dad,' she ran to the massive library and saw all the lovely books, she look through most of the books until she found the perfect book called Skulduggery Pleasant. She sat down on the sofa and stated to read the book.

SWOOSH! She heard behind her, SWOOSH, SWOOSH, 'There it is again I've got to get out of here,' before she could the door slammed shout in front of her, she turned around and a dark figure stood in front of her (SCREAM).

She was never seen again!!!!!!!!!!!!

Jack and the Ghost in Eltham Palace

by Michael Tweneboa - Koduah - age 9

One day the great King announced great news. He wanted every scientist to show him their experiments. It was a science competition and they were all looking forward to it, but one scientist was not quite so happy. His name was Jack Frost and he couldn't think of any experiments. So he went home unhappy.

When he got home it was dark, but then he saw a bright glow in his eyes and shockingly he found a ghost crying. Jack asked the ghost why he was upset. The ghost replied "I am Marco and I need to heat these blue crystals but I can't touch anything, I need someone to heat them for me." Jack looked at the sparkly blue crystals and thought hard. Then suddenly he had an idea! Jack told the ghost that he could help, but only if Marco did a deal with him. Jack said "I will bring a heater and the blue crystals to the palace and I'll heat them, you will turn solid and will be able to touch things again…….deal?" "Deal!" said Marco quickly.

The day finally arrived and everything was in place. Jack had brought the heater and the blue crystals with him and the ghost was right beside him. He was the last person to show the King his experiment. So Jack heated the crystals and the ghost appeared, but was solid. He could touch things again!

Then the King arrived to announce the winner. "Ladies and Gentlemen….. the winner is….Jack Frost!" Everyone clapped and cheered as Jack came on the stage. The King gave Jack a shiny, golden trophy. But then Jack gave the trophy to Marco so he would always be happy. Marco thanked Jack and they all went home and lived happily ever after.

The Haunted Library
by Molly Piller - age 11

It was play time at Middle Park, it was bright day. Unfortunately Jessie and Emma were getting told off by Mr Kilt. "You very naughty girls!" You should not talk in lessons". "We are very sorry", said the girls sadly. The girls got on with their work but soon Mr Kilt sent the girls to the library. They shivered with fear, because the older kids always told the about the Mysteries of Grey Lady......

When they got to the library they noticed there was a mirror. Then they heard a sound, they also heard someone say…."Jessie, Emma, Jessie, Emma", they shook with fear. They decided to look in the mirror and say "Grey Lady" three times. They saw her behind them, slowly they turned around. She was gone......

The girls were reading a book, but suddenly the library started getting colder and colder. They hung onto each other terrified.

Soon enough Grey Lady appeared. She quickly took their souls and the girls were never to be seen again. Their families were sentenced to death for their murders.

But now Grey Lady's grave has risen.

The Tidal Wave

by Nathan Mansfield - age 11

As I peacefully dreamt I see a wave. Not any normal wave, a tall wave. It looked like a tidal wave and it was in the middle of Eltham. It was engulfing cars, traffic and even some buildings. We had nowhere to run and it was just getting bigger every time it ate. When it swished me up I woke up and realised it was a dream so I had a casual day working at The Shard. Then my computer popped up with some news report saying there will be a small bit of rain with some sunny spells. So I went up to the balcony and the skies went dark and by dark I mean you could not even see your hand. Then the rain poured. Not like spitting, like a bucket of water was being thrown and this bucket was big. I guess the news does make mistakes. It lasted a long ten minutes and when I looked over the balcony it infested the roads which sent cold shivers down my spine. Then I worried about my two children beautiful Kyle and Anna. I walked inside and said to my boss that I was going home. My boss replied, "After you do your papers."

"I am going home."

"Fine you're fired!"

As I tried to get to my family a man said, "No entry."

"But I have to get to my family."

"Your choice."

I walked to my house in puddles of water, I opened the door and water nearly picked me off my feet. I saw scratches on the wall which made me scared. I saw a picture of my family cracked in a puddle. I walked up the soaked stairs and saw more scratches on the wall and opened the door and saw a terrible sight.

The Murder on the Train

by James Double - age 10

It started on a cold winter's morning, the land was frosted, the air bitter. One man sat at Eltham station. A train flew past and he was gone! There was nothing to be seen moving apart from the swaying of the trees and the iced-up train. Blood lay on the floor. Something had taken place on the train but who had caused it, and where will they strike next?

The driver on the train heard the commotion and stopped the train to ventured forth into the unknown... the first carriage was empty, just the wind and his footsteps making a sound. The driver then wandered forward and nervously went into the second carriage. Again, empty. Only the faint sound of a fly buzzing around one of the windows made a sound. Then, the final carriage stood there, in front of his eyes. The door opened and he was scared stiff. The wooden plank of a driver had to see what had happened so he manned up and walked in with a nervous grin.

As he got ever closer, the hair on the back of his neck stood up. Two men sat there, one eating a burger, one asleep. At first the driver thought that he was dead. Then, the man snored and a smile filled his face. The driver skipped happily back to his seat. The blood had turned out to be tomato sauce. With the whole mystery solved, the train began to move again. Then, the train stopped at Eltham station. It was rush hour and the station was packed, the burger-eater was getting off and as he did, a man dropped dead on the floor...

Ghost in the Graveyard

by Yad Abdullah - age 10

My friends dared me to stay at the graveyard all night. I accepted the challenge and went there, and that's when it began!

It was a clear night; the moon sparkled through the clouds. I began to lie down and have some snacks; just then I heard footsteps coming closer. I got up and shouted, "You can't scare me Jason".

The clock struck 12o'clock, the door opened by hidden hands, I heard whispers saying "come, come". I hesitantly walked towards the dusty old door. The ancient door shut behind me. I got goose-bumps all over my arms; the ghost held my shoulder and whispered, "I'm coming".

I rushed to the door; it was closed, everything went black, darkness surrounded me. I had no choice but to break the windows and jump out. I grabbed a chair, broke the window, I jumped out and shouted, "help, help, HELP", my voice echoed through the streets but no one replied.

I stopped; it was silent, no one was there, no cars, nothing! I didn't complete the challenge and never will. The ghost made sure of that!!!!!!!!!

ALIEN
by Zaina Kadir - age 8

Once I was walking down an empty road in Eltham and I wondered where everyone was but then I came across an ice-cream van. I asked for some ice-cream but then with a big a big ice-cream it sucked me up and I landed on a pile of people. The van drove to a spacecraft. We got on the spacecraft and we saw some aliens. The spacecraft took off into the, dark, gloomy sky. When the spacecraft stopped and we stepped out we were in Mars. It was a dark red, dusty and smelt of rotten spinach so we ran through alien city and bumped into the alien king. He was quick to shout but this shout was furious. He was smelly, dark green, wrinkly, feeble and ugly. He wanted to roast and eat us so we ran into an army of aliens. They had ten eyes which had an evil look they pushed us on the edge of a platform which lead to a big tray of lava and in the lava was a slimy, ugly monster who wanted him for his lunch. We started to fall into the lava but then a girl alien grabbed us and took us to her spacecraft and we took off but behind us was a group of aliens. We had boosters to make us go faster. We landed in Eltham High Street but all you could see was dust. The aliens were already here but there was a gun which made everything back to normal. It was zapping everything back to normal but the aliens took us back to Mars. We got pushed back onto the platform to the lava. The monster was starting to get hungry so the aliens pushed faster we lost our balance and the monster ate us. He's fat now but the aliens went back to Eltham. END!

Eltham
by Zohra Amiri - age 9

The sun was blazing on my eyes and I was walking towards Eltham. When I got there I went to Superdrug and I was testing their new perfumes and lip balms and when I tested one of their perfumes it smelled like red roses and wet grass and because I loved the smell I brought it. When I came out of the shop suddenly, it began to rain but the rain wasn't white it was red, thick and also smelly. Everybody had blood all over them. Suspiously, I heard a croaky voice saying "come up here" as I was walking towards pound land my feet's started to lift up from the ground when I called for help nobody me. Then I saw 3 wrinkly faces staring at me when I walked closer to the 3 hags I heard a voice saying "you'll turn into a horse" but when I walked backwards I also heard a voice saying "you'll die". I thought to my self why am I going to die and because I thought about it so hard I nearly did turn into a horse. "Why would I turn into a horse" I asked first witch who was stroking her long, rough chin because you didn't do what you were asked to do" "then why am I going to die" I asked the second witch who was looking at me with her blind purply eyes "because you didn't care about anyone" I did" I whispered to myself. Then something smelled very strange I looked around myself and I saw something pink and bubbly. "Do you want to turn into a horse or do you want to die" "ehhhh I don't know "we'll choose then after a few minutes they decided to do nothing.

The Time Machine
by Cara Cloke - age 9

Once upon a time there were 6 children playing in a park in Eltham. They went into Sainsbury's. After they went to the chocolate isle and took all of the chocolate off of the shelf. At the way back they saw something shining, it was a time machine.

The time machine took you back to the old times. They went back to their house and set it back to Tudor times. Cara, Brooke, Shamma and Zaina leaped into the time machine and went to find Queen Elizabeth. When they got there, they saw the wonderful Sir Walter Rahlie and all of Queen Elizabeth's dirty slaves. "Hello your majesty" politely said Shamma," hello what is your name?" "my name is Shamma and these are my friends Brooke, Cara and Zaina, we were just wondering if you could show us the way to Eltham Palace" kindly asked Shamma. " Of course I know the way, I'm the Queen" " oh thank you your majesty " replied Shamma,as she ran to tell her friends. Queen Elizabeth walked all the way to Eltham Palace, walked past the guards and walked the girls to the an escape tunnel. She whispered " if you can get out I will be impressed, because nobody has ever got out before " as she slammed the giant, heavy doors shut. Shamma ran to a tunnel and shouted " guys this tunnel goes on forever".

Cara walked up to the wall and looked up and whispered " wait there's a button it says escape tunnel exit " as she stared at the button. " Well press it " moaned Zaina. Woosh the escape tunnel opened, the girls walked through. The tunnel took them to Fairy Hill Park." Wow the tunnel took us back to the park " spoke Brooke. "Right we have to promise that we will never tell anyone about this because they won't believe us" quickly said Cara, " we promise " whispered everyone. Nobody ever told anyone.

The Boy Who Got Blasted Into Space
by Joseph Cerda - age 8

In one of the houses along Dunvegan Road, there was a family who wanted to go to the fun fair. So they went to Eltham Pleasaunce and the child called Ben wanted to go onto the bouncy castle. His generous parents paid £5.00 for him to go on it. As soon as he jumped on, he started to bounce, bounce and bounce. Suddenly a bigger child jumped up beside him and blasted Ben up high into the sky. Everyone just stared at him looking shocked. A few minutes later, Ben was nowhere to be found. Everyone wondered where he had gone. Then, the curious people started chatting.

They started asking questions such as, "where has the boy gone?" or "how could he vanished in just a glance? Meanwhile, at a NASA Space Station, the astronauts noticed a single dot moving towards them. It came bigger and bigger until, SMASH!!! It crashed! NASA was losing control! AAAAAAAAAAAHHHH!!!!!!!!! Get this thing off! So one of the team came out of the space station and was very surprised to see Ben. He gave Ben a helmet before it was too late. A special helmet with oxygen is needed otherwise he won't be able to breathe. They finally got inside and asked him how he got up there. "You could have died! It's astonishing that you had survived!" They were all gobsmacked! "Hey kid, I'll give you this suit, but remember, BE CAREFUL!" So he jumped out cheerfully into space and turned on his jetpack. When he arrived back at Eltham Pleasaunce, everyone was very pleased to see him. A photographer then came and took a picture of Ben standing by the fountain in the park where he landed. Ben's unexpected adventure was a big headline in the News Shopper's paper the following day.

The Secret of Eltham's Fairies
by Marianne Robinson - age 7

When I went to Eltham Palace I saw a tiny thing. It was a fairy, a tiny fairy. She said "I have one secret I would like to tell you. You know the horses behind the palace, they are not horses they are unicorns and at night they shrink so we can ride them".

Just then the garden was filled with fairies and the first fairy said "And I would like to tell you another secret. We only speak to little girls who believe that fairies are real. But if you go down the path behind Eltham Palace in a full moon you might see a unicorn or maybe a fairy."

And every night when there is a full moon I go and see the fairies.

2014 - High Street - Eltham

Eltham Library

Eltham Miscellany

Some stories were not set in the past, ghost or love stories, but about everyday life and events, but using the few words to tell a story.

Musing about life in Eltham at 4am inspired a story we can all relate to, as we can when reading a story about getting lost, luckily with a good outcome.

We had a story about a young mum taking her baby to a music class and another where children are trick and treating. There is an elderly lady moving house and a reluctant gym member being inspired.

Celebrating a football match win was a great Eltham Experience for a seven year old and a birthday party with balloons was 'a day of fun' for a nine year old.

Everyday events but using the language to share with us experiences and feelings give us a final chapter of our book.

The Music and Movement of a New Mum: Baby Dance Club

by Alex Farrow

Ten weeks old and ready to dance, well granted through me. No; I'm not a pushy mum, just keeping up with what's expected, I think? My first challenge of the day, a huge step into Ink & Folly with the buggy. Impress myself with the fluke of getting in; let's call it 'skill' in which I manage. I take the hundreds of layers off Aurora and sit in the circle of new faces on the floor. We dance babies around; give them scarves to 'hold' as they fly up and down, singing "All the colours in the rainbow". I realise I don't know the words. Another thing to add to the list as I smile and make shapes with my mouth. I know socialising is good for her, all the books say so.

Then oh no, what's that smell? Please don't let it by mine, that's the second this morning. Burning face; I didn't bring a change of clothes. What the other mum's will think? They obviously know more than me. A coffee break, the heavenly sanctum and nectar of all new mums. Finally we chat; a mother slips calling her baby chubby! Is that allowed? Oh what a rush to know these other women are just like me.

We settle back in the circle, a little more at ease, babies cry and another throws up. Is it wrong that this again made me feel better? My stress levels rise again as class ends. It's raining outside, of course no brolley for me, unlike Aurora all wrapped cosy under waterproof canvas. An invite for coffee after at Eltham Centre café, nervous but glad to accept. These women, now friends have grown just as I each day. Still getting it right, or wrong with a smile in our own unique way.

The Move
by Pat Duffy

Eltham is a big place with many people. When Mary moved there she was already in her mid eighties. She couldn't manage the stairs in her flats anymore. She thought she had better move while she was still able. Her children helped her but she still found it upsetting sorting through thirty years worth of accumulated belongings. Her new flat, on the ground floor, was compact and convenient but only had room for essentials. This was good, she thought, putting on a brave smile, a chance to get rid of all the clutter.

She settled in fine. Her children got the place nicely decorated and carpeted, fitted the tiny kitchen out with new units and boiler and she was all set.

Mary was a very bright, capable lady, used to being independent. She sewed and knitted and kept herself busy. She went to Sainsbury's and bought fresh food, which she cooked for herself. She was economical and careful and managed, just about, on her pension. But, there was something missing. All her own friends, who she visited from time to time by bus, lived back near her old flat. Too far for her to travel often. One day her daughter took her to an old people's lunch club nearby. There, to her surprise, she met two of her neighbours from her flats. Why don't you come down with us, they said. We come every week. So Mary started going with them and they became very good friends. A little later she joined some knitting groups where, with her knitting and sewing skills and friendly manner, she made other good friends. Today at ninety-two, she is active and healthy and enjoys life. A good role-model for us younger Eltham residents.

Awake Again
by Angela Sach

It's 4 o'clock in the morning and I'm wide awake. Again. What wakes me at this time of night? How many nights do I lie awake asking why? Silently floating in and out sleep, the times like this make me think about my busy life. I try to see the bigger picture of it all.

I remember the chitter chatter in the school playground. "The lady with her huskies and trap was out for a late night training session again – perhaps she's preparing for the world championship?" says an ambitious little girl. Maybe she could be the reason for my crumbly sleeps.

I recall the considered and judgemental conversation at church; a coffee in my humble hands (Fair Trade, ground of course). Is it the hooligans out joyriding, enjoying the newly laid speed humps in the road?

I recollect people gossiping around me in the supermarket queue. The police helicopter was out again last night, hunting the latest burglar escaping down the A2 in the stolen Porsche 911 – perhaps that is the reason for my late night awakening?

The neighbours are out again now; its spring and we are out of hibernation, cleaning our cars on a Sunday afternoon. The local gossip is about a teenager hiding in the gardens with a knife being chased by an overzealous young constable jumping about in the bushes. A car alarm set off by one of a thousand cats that live round here?

A power cut, a reset timer on the boiler; it's not 4am in Boiler Land but 6am and time to get started, time to fire up the engines and clank the pipes. My life in Eltham is way too exciting to wake me up in the early hours but the homely sound of the boiler? That would be it.

My Story
by Jack Warde - age 7

One day I went to see my brother play football in Eltham. His team won 3-1. When they scored their third goal the ball hit the goalie on the head and knocked him down, but the ball still went in. The goalie had to be carried off the pitch while everybody was still cheering at the team scoring. There was a lot of people there and my brother ran up and down the pitch hi-fiving his team. Afterwards my dad brought us to pizza hut in Eltham to celebrate my brother Paddy winning. We had a large pizza and a lot of juice. Then we had ice cream and we added our own toppings, we had chocolate sauce, M&M's and hundreds and thousands!

Trick or Treat?
by Heaven Osmani - age 9

Five kids were giggling as they ran house to house in Eltham. It was the best time they had had in months. It had stopped raining for the first time in months.

"Trick or treat?" said the kids, going through Eltham, everyone said they looked amazing. They saw weird things going on in the old graveyard. They couldn't stop looking. They felt so scared their hair started to stand up.

Lights were changing quickly. "We should go home," said Rose shivering with fear. "Naah!" replied Daniel.

It started to get cold.

Knocking on the door of the house near the graveyard, the lights were off. They went inside, it was dark and gloomy. The children crept up the stairs. Four of the children disappeared.

Rose stood, all alone, terrified. "Hello, anyone there?" called Rose. She tried to open the doors but they were all locked. She started to cry. One of the windows was open. Rose tried climbing out of the window bur she couldn't get out. Looking around the room Rose found a bed, it was really dusty. Slowly pulling the covers back Rose found a key; it went with the front door. Rose felt relieved, she opened the door. She saw her friends, they started to laugh, they played a trick on her all the time.

Resolution
by Roberta Woods

The gym, yes she would join the gym, this was Nikki's recurring 'New Year's Resolution' which like all such 'resolutions' was soon forgotten as the pounds piled on. This year was different, the new Eltham Centre, with its state-of-the-art gym was just a short walk up Archery Road, no more excuses, she would sign up today. And so, to Peacock's in the High Street - a T shirt, some track-suit bottoms, the requisite 'induction' and henceforth, Mondays, Wednesdays and Fridays would be 'gym' days. Amongst the ageing Baby Boomers priding themselves on their strength and fitness and the young Millenials, their tattoos and capacity to lift heavy weights while admiring their reflection in the mirror, Nikki soon noticed one regular; forty-something, with crutches, he seemed to be there most days quietly doing his 'workout'. Two years passed and still the crutches– 'it cannot simply be a broken leg' Nikki told herself, 'it would have healed by now' however she was too polite to ask.

A 9 month contract job in Canary Wharf temporarily interrupted the gym sessions but all too soon Nikki found herself back on the gym treadmill where she immediately noticed the forty-something man of the previous two years, but now without crutches – this was miraculous - she really had to ask him his story. He had broken his back, not in the usual dramatic manner, simply getting out of bed one day - this horrible crunching noise and he just knew it had gone. On-going back problems had followed his years as a professional footballer but he had been oblivious to the extent of the damage. Several operations later and then the devastating news from the medics that he would probably never walk again. However he had resolved to prove them wrong and after two years hard work at the gym he had done just that.

Nikki felt humbled – now that is what I call Resolution!

HELP???
by Ruby O'Connor - age 9

One hot summer's day, Zara and her brother Johnny decided to go to Eltham Palace. So they set off but they got lost. They asked a tall slim lady if she knew the way there. "Excuse me madam, please may I ask if you know the way to Eltham Palace?" and she muttered "just along there, round the bend and left". So they went the way the lady told them to go and Johnny raged "OH MY GOSH THIS IS NOT ELTHAM PALACE". "Calm down Johnny" said Zara. Zara asked a broad shouldered man if he knew the way there. The man said "just over there". But he was wrong! They found themselves at Eltham High street. "Let's go this way "said Zara begrudgingly, so that's where they went and finally they were at Eltham Palace. Zara read a sign, it said 'ELTHAM PALACE. COME HERE TO LEARN LOTS OF HISTORY AND AT THE SAME TIME HAVE FUN'. "Good, we are here" they chorused and they went in and had a great time.

An Eltham Party

by Molly Warde - age 9

One day I went to a party in Mc Donalds in Eltham. I got a happy meal, because I am a happy child. We had balloons and we tied a load of balloons onto my little sister Ruby and told her she would fly if we tied enough balloons to her.

We lifted her slightly off of the floor and she thought that she was flying! All the people in Mc Donalds laughed and cheered. We had our faces painted as well and Ruby's was painted as a bumble-bee and she was buzzing like one! Then we went home and told my mum and dad all about our day of fun in Eltham.

Eltham Palace

Eltham Palace

Made in the USA
Charleston, SC
04 October 2014